So Much Blue

So Much Blue

A Novel

Percival Everett

Graywolf Press

This publication is made possible, in part, by the voters of Minnesota
through a Minnesota State Arts Board Operating Support grant,
thanks to a legislative appropriation from the arts and cultural
heritage fund, and through grants from the National Endowment for
the Arts and the Wells Fargo Foundation. Significant support has also
been provided by Target, the McKnight Foundation, the Amazon
Literary Partnership, and other generous contributions from
foundations, corporations, and individuals. To these organizations
and individuals we offer our heartfelt thanks.

Published by Graywolf Press
212 Third Avenue North, Suite 485
Minneapolis, Minnesota 55401

www.graywolfpress.org

Published in the United States of America

ISBN 978-1-55597-782-5

6 8 10 12 11 9 7

Library of Congress Control Number: 2016951421

Cover design: Kapo Ng

Cover art: Shutterstock

For Melanie, who has made so much happen

A picture is a secret about a secret.

—Diane Arbus

So Much Blue

I WILL BEGIN WITH DIMENSIONS. As one should. I had a mathematician friend tell me once, perhaps twice, that dimension is concerned with the constituent structure of all space and its relation to time. I did not understand this statement and still I do not, in spite of its undeniable, obvious poetic charm. He also tried to tell me that the dimensions of an object are independent of the space in which that object is embedded. It's not clear to me that even he understood what he was saying, though he seemed quite taken with the idea. What I do understand is that my canvas is twelve feet high and twenty-one feet and three inches across. I cannot explain the three inches, but can say that they are crucial to the work. It is nailed to a wall that is twenty feet tall and thirty-five feet across. The opposite wall is the same and the adjacent walls are but fifteen feet wide. And so the square footage of the space is five hundred twenty-five. The volume of the building space is ten thousand five hundred cubic feet. I am six feet tall and weigh one hundred and ninety-two pounds. I cannot explain the two pounds. I prefer that numbers be written out as words.

I also favor referring to colors by name rather than by sample. I do not like charts depicting gradations of colors or hues. At the paint store or art shop there are thousands of such strips, just waiting to be thrown away. They tell me nothing. The examples, and they are never exemplars or nonpareils, are but mere approximations of what the paint will be on the pallet or on the canvas or the paper or the wood or my fingertips. Transparent yellow is not transparent on the *swatch*. What a word that is. Swatch. Indian yellow might as well be cadmium orange. Aureolin might as well be nickel titanate might as well be lemon yellow. Names, on the other hand, are precise, unambiguous; one might even say rigid, fixed, unalterable,

certainly inelastic. That is not to say that words are not precise, but
names in fact are. Even when they are wrong or offered in error.
A name is never wide of the mark. I should point out that I view
color names as proper names, in that they give us no information
about the things named but identify those things specifically. Just
as my name works for me, my name being Kevin Pace. There are
probably other Kevin Paces in the world, but our names are not the
same. Perhaps our names have the same name, but the name of my
name is not a proper name.

These are my paints, my colors. Powders mixed with linseed oil.
This is my painting, colors on raw linen. I have used much phthalo
blue, Prussian mixed with indigo. In the upper right hand corner
is cerulean blending into cobalt, maybe bleeding into cobalt. The
colors and their names are everywhere, on everything. The colors
all mean something, though I cannot say what, would not say if
I could. Their names are more descriptive than their presence, as
their presence need not and does not *describe* anything. This is my
painting. It lives in this structure that looks like a foaling barn; I
suppose that it is. No one enters but me. Not my wife. Not my children. Not my best friend Richard.

There is another building in which I make other paintings. Everyone is welcome there. The paintings are available and uncovered
and waiting to be considered, bought, and hung on living room
walls or in bank lobbies. I like them well enough. Some are good.
Some not so. It's really not up to me to judge and so I won't. They
are all whores, these paintings. I acknowledge them, appreciate
them as just that. It's not their fault and in fact I do not view that
as a bad thing in and of itself. There really isn't much wrong with
being a whore, if it is done well and without apology or qualifica-
tion. Do they, these paintings that I seem to reference with some
insouciance, though that is not my intention, have some leitmotif?
Maybe. I don't know or care. I wonder if they share anything at all
series to series, canvas to canvas. Experts some years down the pike

will argue about my materials, about my technique, about my palette. I would love to think that there is some of me consistently present on each canvas, then I wonder why it matters, why, to mix metaphors, anyone needs to hear some haunting sequence of notes again and again.

I had a rather brief period of success some years ago. And so I have a bit of money, enough anyway for my family to live comfortably. I send my kids off to private school, though I don't know why. The public school is no doubt better, but it's several miles farther away. The insinuation here is that I am lazy. True enough. Many of their schoolmates seem stupid to me, but perhaps they are merely spoiled. But they are just children. Maybe all children are stupid or maybe they are all geniuses and perhaps there is no difference between the two. Personally, I no longer care about genius. I might have gotten close to it once, but probably not. Who knows? Finally, more importantly, who cares?

My canvas, my private painting, has a title, a name. It has never been spoken aloud to anyone. I have said it only once, under my breath while I was alone in my studio. It is a bit like my email password except that it cannot be retrieved if I forget it. I have not written it down. One reason I will never let my children see the painting is that they might try to name it and so ruin it and everything. I will not let my wife see it because she will become jealous and that will ruin it and everything. I know that my family and friends, though they love me, I imagine, whatever that means, are somewhat eagerly anticipating my death or, just because I love the word, quietus. They all want to see the canvas. I wish I could see their faces if they do, but they will not. They all believe that I do not trust them. This is true enough. They are insulted by the many locks and by the sealed-up windows of the painting's house. I do not trust them as far as I can throw the lot of them collectively. Early on they would occasionally nose around my studio, trying to sneak peeks, even whiffs. Coyotes and raccoons around a tent. They have given up. For now. Is this my masterpiece? Perhaps. Probably not. I don't know what that word means. This notion of a masterpiece has something to do with eternity, forever, I am told. I will have no truck with such concepts, not out of philosophical principle, but as a matter of taste. It may well be that the eternity of a master-piece allows it to exist out of time, but I am too dumb to understand this and not smart enough to refuse to understand it. My *masterpiece* is apparently of great concern to so many. It is not a good feeling to know that one is more interesting dead than alive, but neither is it a terribly bad feeling.

I am fifty-six years old. I saved that dimension for last for no par-ticular, significant, or interesting reason. I am not old by current standards. Sixty is the new forty. Seventy is the new fifty. Dead is the new eighty. That is to say that if I died today everyone would comment on my youth and yet if I broke my leg trying to leap the back fence everyone would call me an old fool. I cannot do many of the things I could once do, but then I don't want to do those things. I have little desire to sprint anywhere or to swim across a river or to dunk a basketball, not that I ever could. But I am in age limbo, too aged to be reckless, too young to be a curmudgeon and get away with it. Yet I am close enough to the other end, the far end of my time line, my expiry date, to generate interest in my work.

There is much talk or chatter, prattling, in the so-called art world (which is more doubtful, *art* or *world*?) about my secret paint-ing, that painting, this painting. I have heard a rumor, canard, if you will allow that term, that some parties are already bidding on it. That tells me all I need to know about *some* parties, *those* people or perhaps about all people. The painting could be ugly. The work could be shoddily made. It could be insulting, shallow, morally re-pugnant, silly, or, worst of all, pedantic. From what I have heard, my family might be taken care of for a couple of generations after my death. There is really nothing comforting in this knowledge. None of it will happen anyway. My best friend, a retired Beowulf scholar named Richard, has promised me that he will burn the studio to the ground if I should die before him. I believe he will be faithful to this promise, but sadly I doubt that he will outlive me. And so I have a plan to booby-trap the place. But first I have to figure out how to do it without harming anyone, especially myself. It's not that I do not trust Richard, it's that I do not trust traffic. I do not trust the weather. I do not trust lines of communication, fiber optics and microwaves notwithstanding. Neither do I trust automobiles, especially those without carburetors. Richard might be on vacation or flirting with a woman he's met on the village square when I die of a sudden. Mobile reception might be lost because of a lightning strike to a tower. It could happen. I know that Richard will do his best and will get it done if he has the chance. I know he will do it because he is my friend.

I take friendship very seriously. If you are my friend and you need me then I will find you. I will be there even if it means bringing a bicycle chain to a fight in an alley at two in the morning. That may sound extreme, but this is how I am. Moreover, I attract friends who think like me. I'm not saying it's a good thing, but it is a thing. Richard will burn my studio to the ground because we are friends, not because of what happened thirty years ago.

This might seem like a likely or predictable segue for me to offer the story of what happened thirty years ago. I will tell you that, but not yet. First, I will tell you what happened ten years ago.

My wife and I were in Paris for a couple of weeks. It was supposed to be a romantic getaway, without the kids, a nice warm time to celebrate twenty years of perfectly fine, loving, safe marriage. And it was so a romantic time, however, alas, with someone else. In itself this is not a startling admission. Neither is it exceptional that my affair was with a twenty-two-year-old aspiring watercolorist. Surprising, but not exceptional. The only thing extraordinary is that I would admit to something so pathetically clichéd. It happened after my wife decided, and I encouraged her, innocently, to spend a couple of days in Bordeaux with her college roommate. That is the story I will tell you now. It is a story about being old and about being young.

First cliché, I loved and love my wife, was not bored with her, was not unhappy with my life, with my children, or with my work. I was not looking for excitement or adventure or even sex, though all three have their appeal. It started in a silly way, like something out of junior high school, too tame to be a male fantasy, literally a brush of hands, a light rake of skin that persisted at first a beat too long and then was revisited. Like most things that come back to haunt you, it haunted me in the beginning. No ghost is born overnight.

I had never thought much one way or another about being a cliché. In my profession, as an artist, I might well have been just that. I was somewhat introverted, a little odd to many, a lot odd to some, moody, mildly sloppy in dress, absentminded. I possibly cut a handsome figure in my youth, as my mother might have said, but that never mattered to me, and it is more than possible that it was not true at all. It turns out that one becomes a cliché from inattention. I was not observant, was not taking in my surrounds fully.

I wandered into a little lecture at the museum at the Jardin du Luxembourg. On the walls behind the clearly articulating docent dressed like a flight attendant were some thirty paintings by Eugène Boudin. They were all of cows, of course. I was impressed by this fact; so many cows. I was completely bored by the paintings, but excited to be able to follow the lecture in French.

I was sitting next to a young woman with perhaps the whitest skin I had ever seen. She was attractive, I suppose. I didn't think about this at the time. It had been many years since I had thought about whether someone was attractive or not. I considered that she might have been the only actual white person I had ever seen, a pedestrian thought, but honest enough. Yet she did not look like

the porcelain doll one hears so much about. Was she zinc white?
Titanium? I decided she was flake white, with all its lead danger.
Her hair was light blond, but that hardly mattered. We were sitting on a backless bench. I gripped the seat on either side of me and
leaned slightly forward. It turned out she was gripping the bench as
well, her left hand next to my right. The backs of our hands grazed.
I looked at her and said, *"Pardon,"* and moved my hand away an
inch. Then, either by her conscious or unconscious movement, by
my conscious or unconscious movement, by an anomaly of gravita-
tional force, or by the vibrations of the building caused by a distant
metro train, a bus, or a low-flying jet, or the folding of space, our
hands touched again. Dimension. This time neither of us moved
away. Perhaps we were both thinking, so what, our hands are touch-
ing, this won't kill me, it's just where our hands happen to be. But it
felt good. At least to me, so I left it there. I peeked at her and guessed
she was in her twenties and that's when I really felt like a cliché. I
was a dirty old man. Worse, I was a dirty old artist man.

After the lecture everyone wandered about staring dumbly at
all the portraits of cattle. I felt a bit of sadness thinking about the
paintings that way, perhaps shame. They were rather nice pictures
of cows, but I could not tell one from the next. Who could? I doubt
a cow could. My boredom must have shown on my face because
the young woman with the hand stood next to me and said, "You
don't like them."

I looked at her.

"It's not that," I said. "Not exactly anyway."

She questioned me.

"Really, I get it that he inspired Monet and all that. I love the
paint and painting. I do. It's that, well, wouldn't twelve have been
enough?"

"I don't understand," she said.

"Wouldn't twelve paintings of cows have been enough?" I felt
silly repeating it. "Perhaps he didn't want some cows to feel slighted."

"I do not understand *slighted*," she said.

I searched. "*Négligé?*"

She nodded. "*Vous êtes drôle.*"

"I try. I apologize for my French. *Je suis désolé.*"

"It is okay. I speak English. But I have an accent."

"The accent is nice."

"Americans always say that."

"Do we?"

"I don't know," she said. "I'm not very good at flirting with old men."

She was lying. I felt like an old fool just talking to her, though I had no designs. I would have been less of a cliché if I had had some designs. I would sound like less of one now if I admitted to having had designs, but I was what I was. As much as it pained me to admit, in a moment of reducing myself to an artistic expression, I resigned myself to a kind of Greenbergian complaint about surrealism, my present cliché being just that, surrealistic, that the picture fails because of an appeal to the anecdotal. An equally painful admission was that I believed, as much as I did not want to, that the medium was everything. Canvas and paint, that's all there was, all there is. The medium there, in that museum, of my cliché, was two bodies. And sad as it made me, and excited as well, I knew that the two bodies would find each other. It wasn't male fantasy; I was never confident enough for that. It was artistic prescience, if that makes any sense. Even if it doesn't, that's what it was.

"Are you an artist?" she asked.

"I am. I'm a painter, an old-fashioned painter." I said this even though I had no idea what I meant. I never offered my profession any amount of second-order thinking or consideration. I had one prolonged and pointedly tiring argument with some idiot from the Yale English department about whether painting was a language. Without asking what I know now to be the correct and reasonable response—which was "Huh?"—I instead said, "Why of course it is." He said something about art not being able to write its own grammar, but rather betrays it in its invention. My response to this was cognac. And when I was good and drunk, I said, "A painting is not meant to signify, but to show." When I saw him on his heels from my first salvo of nonsense I finished him off with "The semantic function of a painting is not a criterion of its aesthetic quality." The hit was complete. Had I been a real mafioso I would have then slept with his wife.

"And what do you try to make when you paint?" the young woman asked me. She was not tilting her head in a certain way, but I noticed it.

"I'd be happy to make a cow, " I said.

She smiled, verged on a sound.

"I'll tell you what I want to paint. I want to make a painting and have no idea what it is, but know that it's a painting. Does that make sense to you?"

"Maybe if you said it in French."

"I doubt that would help."

"You're noticing the way I walk," she said.

I hadn't, but I nodded anyway.

"It's the walk I save for old men."

"You practice it?" I asked.

"It comes naturally."

"I believe you."

"I too am a painter. I make watercolors."

"I don't have that kind of control. Too much thinking up front."

Since she'd mentioned her walk I could not fail to pay attention to it. She bounced and wore her youth aggressively. She was beautiful. Her face didn't matter. Her body didn't matter. Anyone walking like that had to be beautiful. Every turn, every stop, every start was choreographed and yet completely free, improvised. She was jazz and I could have hated her for it, but I did not.

"*Voulez-vous vous joindre à moi pour le café?*"

"*Alors formelle,*" she said.

"I'm sorry, my French isn't good enough to give you *tu* easily."

"Your French is cute."

"I get a headache trying to speak French," I told her. "Especially listening. I don't hear the language well."

"Pity," she said.

The word *pity* had never meant so much and perhaps so little as it did from her lips at that moment. The word itself, the two sounds of it, more so than the meaning, were not locatable. The word was there all right, but there like an electron is there.

"Yes, I will take coffee with you," she said. "I will practice my English. And you can practice whatever it is you are trying to speak."

"My name is Kevin."

She shook my hand. "Victoire."

Against my better judgment, which is to say that I was exercising no judgment at all, she and I walked from the Jardin du Luxembourg north on rue Bonaparte. We said nothing until we reached the fountain at Saint-Sulpice.

"Are you studying art?" I asked.

"Yes, at the École des Beaux-Arts."

"Impressive."

"Yes, it is," she said and leaned against the low wall of the fountain. It was midafternoon on a mild but windy December day. Mist from the fountain floated in the air. I looked at the statues of lions.

"Let's have that coffee," I said.

She nodded and we walked over to the Café Mairie and sat outside under a heat lamp where the waiter gave me a knowing look that was either approving or disapproving, I could not tell, but either was equally troubling.

"The waiter thinks you're young enough to be my daughter," I said.

"Then he thinks too much," Victoire said.

"At any rate, it's polite of you to sit and talk me."

"And you said you didn't know how to flirt."

"I'm forty-six years old, married with two children, and happy with my life."

"Yet here you are."

"Yet here I am," I repeated.

"I know your work," she said. "I've seen some paintings in magazines. I liked them."

"Photographs of paintings are deceptive. You might not like them in person."

"Perhaps."

Coffee went on as one might have expected. Victoire told me about her watercolors, gently stroked my ego by talking about my own work, did so with the perfect, perhaps French, amount of constraint and then we parted with an agreement to meet for lunch two days later. We managed to end before I stupidly complimented her appearance. It dawned on me, as I wandered north along the busy rue de Rennes on my way to my hotel, that I could have said something like "You're quite lovely." I was at once proud of myself for not thinking to make such a vacuous assertion and dismayed, perhaps embarrassed, that I considered it even after the fact.

That night my wife called from Bordeaux. Linda told me she was enjoying her friend, but not so much Bordeaux. I told her about my coffee with the twenty-two-year-old.

"That's wonderful," she said. "I'm glad you got out. It's good to meet people."

"We sat at the Café Mairie."

"Was she beautiful?"

It pained me to have to consider what might be an appropriate response, so I did what I always did, out of a lack of imagination, lack of a gauge of political delicacy, lack of a decent memory, I told the truth. "Yes, she was."

"That's wonderful."

I nodded, though on the phone.

"I'm having lunch with her on Friday."

"Just so long as you're not late meeting my train."

"Montparnasse?"

"*Oui, quatre heures.*" And with that Linda had exhausted her French and ended our conversation. "Good night," she said.

"Night."

That illusions are a physical fact is difficult to reconcile with the knowledge that reality is anything but real. All that I will tell you is true, but I have no idea what true is. I come by my ignorance honestly, perception beginning and ending at the same neurological point in space. I can tell you that I was still innocent when I hung up the phone that night, and yet I was not.

1979

If only I had had the excuse of misunderstanding why I was there, perhaps then some of the guilt would not exist, perhaps then I would not have blamed myself to this day, perhaps then I would not long for a piece of me that died that day. But my friend had come to me, depressed, fearful, lost, and he had asked for my help. I offered it willingly, if not completely innocently or selflessly. That was thirty years ago. It was May 1979. It might be tempting to suggest that this episode of my life here presented is some kind of playing out of a redemption story, and I do mean that in the most vulgar Christian sense, but that is just so much bullshit.

Richard came to me with a needlessly long story about his brother. Though Tad was older than Richard, Richard comfortably referred to him most of the time as Fup; the *fuckup*. Richard said it was commonly understood, but seldom acknowledged by his family. Fup had been in and out of detention, prison, abusive relationships, and an assortment of drug rehab programs. Tad had shot himself not once, but twice with the same habitually noncleaned pistol on different occasions. Tad was his mother's favorite, a fact Richard read as fair enough given his brother's difficulties, failures, and bad luck. Fup ought to have something, if not common sense or a modicum of good fortune. As it was reported to me, Richard's mother had not heard from Tad in seven months and upon calling his last known number she was told that he was last headed for El Salvador. She did not think to ask why he was headed there, but was alarmed nonetheless. This alarm was of course well placed and of course affected badly the youngest child, a bipolar, anorexic German-language major still living at home, to the point that she was suicidal and this of course led Richard to believe that he had to do something, namely, find Tad. He asked me to go with him. Richard is my friend.

We were both twenty-four and probably, technically, insane or at least not in our right minds. Richard and I were both in our third year of graduate school at Penn, he in the middle of his dissertation on Beowulf, I in the middle of pretending I could pretend to be a painter, sharing a small, run-down house on Baltimore Avenue. It was a rough neighborhood in which I felt safe enough, though the house was set far too close to the busy street, because the house looked like shit, a hovel, and because it was therefore obvious that we had nothing worth stealing. Richard claimed to feel secure because I was black, not that he believed I could or would protect him, but because everyone else in the neighborhood was black and he felt that by mere association he was more accepted. I told him to shut up.

"I don't really understand," I said. We were sitting in our near-furnitureless living room on the bench in the bay window, watching some firemen attempt to stay clear of a crack addict from central casting who was swinging a shovel, guarding a wheelbarrow of something that was on fire. "Just how do you know Tad's in El Salvador?"

"His friends told my mother he was going there. Then I called the State Department," Richard said.

"And they just up and told you he was there?" The sweeping red light from the fire truck was giving me a headache.

"No, they said, 'Who are you and why do you want to know?'"

"Pretty much an admission."

"Pretty much."

"So what do you want to do?" I asked.

"He must have run into some kind of trouble. Maybe he's in a jail cell and needs a lawyer. Maybe he's in a hospital and can't remember his name. Who knows? I need to go down there and see if I can find him. My mother and sister will go crazy. Crazier. Will you go with me?"

"El Salvador," I said. "That's far away. Man, just how hot do you suppose it is down there?"

"Low nineties. I checked."

"That's doesn't sound so bad," I said. It didn't take a genius to see this was not a good proposition, but it did take an idiot to not see it. "Okay, I'll go, but I don't like it. Wouldn't you rather be working on your dissertation?"

"This is more important. This is my brother. Here's your ticket." He handed me a Pan Am ticket jacket. "We change planes in Miami."

I looked at the ticket. I liked the Pan Am logo, the blue and the white. "And just what would you have done if I had said no?"

"Never occurred to me."

I always wondered, even as a child, and, from all reports, I was not an overly bright one, if there is a difference between good sense and common sense. Nous. I assume that common sense is not the sort of thing that requires specialized knowledge whereas good sense might. My father contended that common sense has nothing to do with good sense, just as common fashion has nothing to do with taste. One might have the common sense necessary to see a painting as a waste or abuse of pigments, linseed oil, and linen, but not have the good sense to buy it. It was clear to me as I packed a bag that I was practicing neither.

Ilopango Airport was small and acutely busy, looking more like a large bowling alley than anything else. Soldiers, in their olive drab uniforms and camouflage caps, paraded with some swagger back and forth in front of the area where the bags were not mechanically conveyed, but tossed from carts into the middle of the room. We grabbed our bags and walked through the entry point essentially unchecked, but extremely noticed. Our lack of Spanish seemed to annoy people less than I had imagined it would. I sensed certainly that we were filthy Americans and that our age and appearance suggested that we might have been there for a rather limited range of reasons or ventures, but, possibly for that latter reason, we buzzed through customs with merely a nod and still-zipped duffels. As I passed the point, as my passport was stamped with only a fleeting, but no less reproving, glance, I had the feeling that I had been there before, that I would be there again, not in that country, but passing unregistered, however noted, through a station that was memorable, perhaps profound, yet immaterial, but not completely nugatory. Back then, in my more sincere, naive, or wet-behind-the-ears artistic self, I might have chosen the word *unavailing*, the important part being that I would not have cared if I was right or wrong.

Outside, while we waited for a taxi, several kids danced to a blaring tape of the Village People singing "In the Navy."

"That's just wrong," Richard said.

I was sad that I sort of liked it.

The tune was still in my head when the taxi let us out in front of the American Embassy. Annoying as it was, I almost sang the song aloud as I looked across the huge traffic roundabout at a grand fountain. The embassy itself, though large, was not so grand, looking like a rectangular layer cake more than anything else. We showed our passports to a refrigerator-shaped marine who was no more moved by or interested in us than the customs agents had been. He waved us into the compound. Richard told the man at the desk why we were there, that we were looking for his brother, that nothing had been heard from him in months, that the fear was that he might have been arrested and left to rot in a jail or dungeon someplace. It was my opinion that Richard was talking too much, but I didn't interrupt.

We sat for just over an hour before another man came out to us. I thought he looked alarmingly similar to the first man. He was tall, nearly handsome, blond, and he wore an air of dismissal that wafted in front of him like so much cologne. He sat in a chair across from us in the waiting area. Richard repeated his speech about why we were there, but this time he added a bit about the hospital before mentioning that he worried his brother was festering in a cell somewhere.

"And just what might your brother have been arrested for?"

"I don't know if he's been arrested," Richard stammered. "I only offer that as a possibility. We haven't heard from him in so long. He could, as I said, just as well be in a hospital."

"But you did say jail. Why did you think he'd be in jail? Has your brother ever been arrested?"

"Yes."

"Where?"

"In Baltimore. And Philadelphia."

"Boston," I added.

"And yes, Boston," Richard said. "But I don't see what this has to do with anything."

"I see. What was he arrested for?"

Richard let out a long breath and leaned back in his chair. "A couple of times for possession of drugs and once for discharging a firearm."

"What is your brother's name?"

"Tad Scott."

The man leaned forward the way one does when one is about to leave. "I don't see that there is much I can do to help you."

"You can't call around?" Richard asked. "Just check jails and hospitals, something like that?"

"If he was looking for his seventeen-year-old sister who was down here with a Christian youth group from Massachusetts, the niece of a congressman, could you make a few calls then?" I asked.

"Yes, then I could and I probably would make a few calls. I might even give a flying fuck." He looked me in the eye. "Good day, gentlemen."

We watched the man shut the door behind him. "What do you think?" Richard asked.

"I think he's smarter than he looks."

"About my brother."

"I think he's dumber than he looks."

Seated not far from us, having gone not completely unnoticed, but unnoticed enough, until he cleared his throat, was a short, thick

man in a Hawaiian shirt. "I couldn't help but overhear," he said with
a pronounced Southern accent. "I happen to know somebody who
might just be willing able to help you boys out." He handed Richard
a yellow slip of paper that had been torn from a pad. He was rather
obvious about looking around while he talked to us.

"Is this a phone number?" Richard asked.

"Yeah, this guy might be able to help you out right nicely. He's
American, lives just outside the city."

"What is he, a private detective or something?"

"No, he's a *condottiero*."

"A what?"

"A soldier," I said.

Richard looked at me.

"I've seen them in paintings," I said.

"So, he's a mercenary," Richard said.

"Such an ugly word. Anyway, call him, maybe he can offer some
assistance, get you to your brother."

"Do you sit here all day waiting for people like us?" I asked.

"Yes." He went back to reading his magazine.

"What's in this for you?" I asked.

"A public service," he said. "I get mine, don't you worry. Capi-
talism is alive and well."

Richard shoved the paper into his pocket and started for the
door, but I didn't move. I was fixated on the man in the Hawaiian
shirt.

"Come on," Richard said. "What are you looking at?"

I tried to see the cover of the magazine the man was reading. It
was an issue of *Sports Illustrated* and I could see Reggie Jackson on
the cover in an Oakland A's uniform.

"What is it?" Richard asked, pulling me away.

"That magazine is ten years old? He's sitting in here reading a
ten-year-old sports magazine."

"How do you know it's ten years old?"

"Because that was the last time I gave a flying fuck about baseball. The guy's crazy."

"Let's get out of here," Richard said.

I couldn't let it go. I felt strangely irritated. "Hey, you know Reggie Jackson plays with the Yankees now."

Hawaiian shirt looked up, gave me an uninhabited smile, turned the page, and went on reading.

Outside the building a sturdy, red-faced crisp marine informed us that if our business was done we'd have to leave the grounds. We did. If first hours can be considered discouraging, then these were and Richard, more than I, was ready to head straight back to the airport and go home. Though it was ninety degrees and very humid, exactly what we had left in Philadelphia, I found even the weather exotic and I recognized my slipping, if not into adventurousness, then into a state of vacation. The colors were different, more vibrant, whether it was true or not, rich in blues, more cerulean than the blues at home, and yellows, closer to mustard. I was as well taken by the stares we attracted and even then I was embarrassed by both my regard of and my attraction to this attention.

Outside a hotel that we imagined we could afford, only because of its state of disrepair, I passed coins to Richard as he tried to place a call to the number he had been given in the embassy. The word written by the number was *bummer* in all lowercase letters. It might have been a name or a comment, so instead of asking for someone by that name, Richard merely said the word as if it were a password. Richard covered the mouthpiece and said, "His name is Bummer." It didn't take much imagination to see this as a bad sign.

"Some guy at the embassy gave me your number. He said you might be able to help me." Before Richard could begin to describe the situation with his brother, "Wait, let me get a pencil." I handed him a pen and he wrote on the piece of paper, was still writing after he hung up. To me he said, "We need to rent a car."

"Bummer?" I asked.

"Guy sounded scary." Richard made his voice scratchy and tried to mimic the man. "Yeah, I'm the Bummer."

"*The* Bummer?"

"*The* Bummer." He continued in his Bummer voice, "Don't say nothing, just come to this address. Bring me some mangoes."

"No shit?"

"No shit."

In the hotel we were told of a car rental a few blocks away. A few blocks away turned out to be a short trail into an even rougher section of the city. Trash was piled without conscience against walls and into the street. A woman who might have been a prostitute leaned against a derelict car and eyed us as possible clients, though I doubt it in retrospect. It's ever more likely that she saw us as casualties. There was no sign, but a small gravel lot with four cars and an office with a screen door. A man sat at a steel desk, his feet up, and nodded as we entered. He was dressed in a long-sleeved flannel shirt and cowboy boots in spite of the heat and ate from a box of Cracker Jack. "Welcome, gringos," he said in a rehearsed voice and expended what turned out to be the extent of his English. "*Quieres alquilar un auto?*"

"*Auto, sí,*" Richard said.

"*Tengo cuatro que hay.*"

Richard and I looked out at the late-fifties Ford pickup, the battered Bel Air, the Willys Commando, and the '63 Caddy. "*Lleve a su selección.*"

Richard looked at me. "I think he said to pick one."

"The Willys," I said.

"*Pero sólo el Cadillac corre,*" the man said.

"*Qué?*" I said. "What did he say?"

"*El azul,*" Richard said.

The man shook his head. "No run. Only Cadillac."

"Then why did you—" Richard stopped, shook his head.

He looked at me and I said, "If we had some bacon we could have eggs and bacon, if we had some eggs."

"*Cuánto por el Caddy?*" Richard asked.

"*Ciento,*" the man said. "*Un día.*"

"A hundred a day. That's not bad," Richard said.

"*Dólares Americanos*."

"A hundred dollars a day? We don't have that kind of money. *No tenemos mucho*." Richard sighed.

"*Podemos darle diez*," I said. The man frowned at me. I pulled out my pockets to show him that I was poor.

"*Por favor*," Richard said.

"*Quince*," he said.

"Okay," Richard said and put fifteen dollars on the table.

"Deposit," the man said. "*Ciento*."

Richard put a hundred dollars on the desk.

The man did not thank him.

"*Las llaves están adentro*."

"*Gracias*," Richard said.

I thanked him also and we walked out before he could change his mind. He didn't ask for our passports or licenses, just scooped up the money and shoved it in his breast pocket and continued to eat his Cracker Jack.

The blue one, the '63 Caddy Coupe de Ville, was a finned beast that screamed in American English when Richard cranked the engine. There was a hole in the muffler that somehow seemed necessary. Our right turn out of the lot fishtailed a cloud of dust behind us and when I looked through it I saw Cracker Jack watching us from the doorway. We wended our way northeast and out of the city into a rural suburb consisting of clapboard shacks and trailer homes. The Bummer's trailer stood out as the nicest on the block; it had a door. Neighbors, chickens, and a donkey studied us as we knocked on that door.

"Come."

We entered and found a man seated elbows on knees on a built-in sofa against the facing wall. He might have been thirty, but he was worn, his blond hair thin on top, his face oddly clean-shaven. The place smelled of salami and Aqua Velva. The dirty floral cushions curved up around his ass.

"Are you Bummer?" Richard asked.

"I'm the Bummer. Where are my mangoes?"

"We didn't bring them," Richard said.

"I ask these motherfuckers to do one thing and they fuckin' forget," he said as if to someone else. "One motherfuckin' thing."

"Sorry about that," Richard said.

"What's your name?"

"Richard Scott. I'm trying to find my brother."

"Who's he?" The Bummer nodded toward me without actually looking at me. "He your driver?"

"My friend."

"Kevin," I said.

"I don't give half a fuck what your name is," the Bummer said.

"I suppose not," I said.

The Bummer glared at me until I looked away.

"Like I said, I'm trying to find my brother," Richard repeated, his voice high with fear.

"So tell me, Richard Scott, why do you think this brother of yours is here in El Salvador?"

"This is where he said he was headed."

"And just why might he be headed here?" The Bummer lit a filterless Camel and blew the smoke up at the ceiling. "You see, I can't think of any good reason for an American young man to come down here to this goddamn motherfucking asshole of a country."

"You're here," I said.

"Yeah, I'm here," he said without looking at me. "I'm here because I'm a goddamn motherfucking asshole. I'm here because I love to sweat year round. I'm here because I hate faggots like you up in the good ole U.S. of A. I'm here because I miss motherfucking Viet-fucking-nam."

"You're a mercenary," I said.

"Fuck you," the Bummer said and blew smoke at me. "So, tell me about this brother. This brother got a name?"

"Tad."

"Sweet name. Is he a hippie faggot like you two motherfuckers? What does he look like? Tall? Short? Bald?"

"He's thirty-one, about my size. His hair is shorter." Richard looked at me. "He's got a tattoo on the left arm, a tiger and some Chinese ideograms."

"Ideograms," the Bummer repeated and sneered. "What kind of drugs is he into? Does he sell guns?"

"What?" Richard said.

"Come on, stupid. He ain't no missionary come down here to the third world to save greaser souls, so he's either buying drugs or selling guns. My money's on the drugs."

"It probably is drugs," I said.

"Probably." The Bummer chuckled.

Richard began to grow impatient. He bounced on the balls of his feet. "The guy at the embassy said you would be able to help me."

"He's his brother," I said, trying to appeal to some inkling of decency in the man. "He just wants to find his brother." Even though I didn't say it, I left the word *asshole* hanging in the air.

"You got a picture?"

Richard pulled a folded photo from his jacket pocket and handed it to the man. The Bummer didn't examine it, but placed it facedown on the coffee table in front of him.

"What kind of drugs?" the Bummer asked. "What does he like?"

"Cocaine and weed," Richard responded immediately. "That's what he was into before."

"Are you college boys?" the Bummer asked.

We said nothing. I was confused.

"Do you boys go to college?

"Yes," I said.

The Bummer smiled. "What do you take?" He paused. "In college, what do you take?"

"I study art," I said.

His smile broadened. "You're telling me that while I was sweating and pulling rat-sized leeches off my big white dick in shittin' Vietnam you were sketching naked girls in a sunny room?"

"Every chance I got," I said.

My response took him by surprise and his smile changed in

quality. It was oddly less threatening, but it was clear he didn't hate me less. "You know how many gooks I killed over there? Want me to tell you?"

Richard looked at me and I turned and studied the scene outside the window. An older woman was hanging clothes on a line. A young, stocky boy was pushing a small rocking chair across the yard.

"I killed me around a thousand of them. Every fuckin' slant I saw, I killed. What do you girls think about that? About a thousand, give or take a family."

"I think we're in the wrong place," Richard said.

I was proud of Richard in that moment and I was more than ready to leave with him.

"Calm the fuck down," the Bummer said. "Don't get your skivvies all bunched up. I can find your brother. I need to know if you got any money. How much money you got?"

"About a thousand dollars," Richard said.

"Do you have a grand or not?"

"He has a thousand dollars," I said.

The Bummer looked out the window behind Richard and me. "I'll do it for a grand, but only because I like you college boys."

Richard gave me a glance. I shrugged or suggested a shrug.

"You pay me when the job is done," the Bummer said. "How does that sound? Come back here tomorrow morning at seven and we'll get started. You girls know how to wake up early?"

"We'll manage it," I said.

"About you," the Bummer said, pointing his cigarette hand at me.

"Yeah?" I said.

"Don't think I didn't notice that you're a nigger."

"I was afraid you missed that fact?"

"I'm just saying," he said. "I killed some of you over in Nam, too. You know, when nobody was looking. A lot of you motherfuckers over there." He smiled.

"Of course you did. I doubt you could kill anything while some-body was looking."

"We'll be back in the morning," Richard said. He grabbed me by the shoulder and pulled me toward the door.

"Good. Now go on. Squeeze out that morning wood and be here on fucking time."

House

My children had little use for their father beyond the usual business of daily familial maintenance, that much was clear. It was apparent that they were not the best at loving. Since their mother seemed pretty good at it I am afraid that the blame for this deficiency fell squarely on my shoulders, even if I cannot articulate why it was so. My daughter and I were close when she was younger. Then the hormones. My general failure as a father.

Once upon visiting Picasso's museum in Antibes, Matisse stood staring at the *Reclining Woman*. Apparently the odalisque bothered him. He studied the long plywood panel for a while and then said that Picasso had done something odd with her bottom, that the two parts of it turned in a strange way. They don't follow the other planes of her body, he said. He then took out a notebook and made a sketch of the painting which he no doubt took home to study.

It was the same house every summer on Martha's Vineyard. It was not our house, but it was enough ours that it wore marks that were our own, a burned spot on the kitchen counter, a chipped tile on the floor of the shower. One year I was dismayed to find a cracked board of the outdoor shower floor replaced. There were books that we had left there, that had been perused by the other people who rented the house during the other months. A small canvas of mine hung on the wall of the tiny living room. Back before the children were teenagers, the place was happy and full of light. However, as they grew older, tearing them from their friends and their world to be stranded on that island with their mother and father turned out to be difficult for everyone.

Every morning Will and I would canoe out into the middle of

the tidal pond behind the house and sit and watch the ospreys hunt and return to their nests. Once we even got to see a young one fledge. Will was twelve at the time. He became so excited that he jumped up in the canoe and capsized us. My feet sank into the deep silt of the bottom. I grabbed Will by his belt and hoisted him to the shell of the canoe. We were never in any danger and once we were both latched onto the boat we began to laugh hysterically. I righted the canoe, pushed him in, and managed to haul myself in as well. We were soaked but didn't care. Will cared about the osprey only insofar as it was a necessary piece in the story of our capsize. When he got back to the house, he told the story in great detail, laughing harder than before, describing the look on my face, how cold the water felt. April laughed with him at first then she faded into the background. I watched her recession.

There was an old barn on the property, not large, nearly ready to fall over, and I used it for painting. I have to say that I was very happy every month we spent there and yet I had never made a single painting there that I liked even a little bit. Not until that day, that day when I watched my daughter's quiet insecurity, perhaps jealousy, reveal itself. That night I didn't sleep, but opened my notes and composed a small painting, *Fledgling Blue*, that would become the seminal image of my large private painting. My daughter's re-action, as brief, as fleeting, as little revisited as it was, was, I believed, my first actual glimpse of her love for me. I recognized the vanity of my thinking immediately, but that wasn't sufficient to dismiss it. I wanted her to love me as I loved her. I wanted her to love me the way I imagined she loved me when she was little.

On that little canvas, everything I had ever tried to make came together. My desire to understand something about submergence— that was the word I used, thinking it was clear enough to me and knowing that it was completely baffling to others—was replaced with an attempt to create a metaphor for the biological. The edges of my shapes, my lines, they all softened, my colors became less metal, less earth, and became, for lack of a better word, cellular.

The next morning, I awoke before Will, but found April pushing around her cereal at the kitchen table. I sat across from her and poured cereal into my own bowl. Her mother was in the shower.

"Hey, kiddo, I was wondering if you might like to go out in the canoe with me this morning."

"Will is still asleep."

"Will can stay here this morning. You never go out with me. Alone, that is. I thought it would be nice for a change."

"Okay."

We finished breakfast and walked across the wet lawn to the beach and the canoe. April sat down in the front and I pushed us out into the pond. We paddled with the tide out into the middle. Easy going. We stopped out there and just drifted. The ospreys came and went and were as beautiful as ever. We said little, usually, "Look at that one." We never saw the baby. The day grew hot, the sun intense.

"Can we go back now?" April asked.

"Of course."

But paddling back was against the current. I paddled and paddled but could make no headway. April would paddle a few strokes and then become inattentive, willfully distracted, which would have been fine if she hadn't left her idle paddle in the water and so turned us every time. It took three times as long to fight the current and get us back to our beach.

Will met us as we approached the house. He was excited that we had been out. "Did you see the baby?" he asked.

April walked by without looking at him, said in flat, hollow voice just loud enough to be heard, "Fuck you."

Apparently the aging Monet lost confidence in his late works and wanted to set fire to them. What patience he must have had to wait until he was old to feel that. And oh the differences in our problems, Monet and I. He was struggling with how to make the paint render clear water with grass moving beneath the surface. I struggled to understand why the fuck I was painting. I recalled my grandfather seeing one of my early paintings just before his death. It was a medium-sized canvas, perhaps three by four feet, with lots of greens and blues, the colors applied beside each other in rough, quick strokes, a sphere of ocher and Indian yellow loosely mixed with white trying to erupt near the center. Stenciled across the bottom of the canvas in a fairly straight line was the word *depiction* in lowercase letters. My grandfather smiled at me, said, "I like it. But Kevin, do any roads lead home from irony?"

Years earlier, when the children had a bedtime, Linda and I found our way to the porch once they were put down. I was still smoking at the time and also still drinking and I might have been a little drunk. I lit my cigar in the dark. The red-orange glow of it made me want to paint. Linda was wearing her hair tied tightly back, the way I'd told her I liked. Long ago when I'd asked her to marry me I think it was my deep sadness and melancholy that made her say yes. She was a romantic and I suspect she thought she could save me. I suppose I thought the same.

"Look at the fireflies," Linda said.

I watched the insects. "There are far fewer than there used to be. What do you think that means?" I asked.

"I don't know."

"End of the world maybe," I said.

And suddenly, as if to prove me wrong, nature put a riot of fireflies in front of us. They were marvelous and I felt small. "Or maybe we'll live forever," I said.

"Cool," Linda said.

"Cool?"

"Too much time with Will."

"So, tell me, when did you know you loved me?" I asked.

"I know exactly the moment I fell in love with you. We were in that little bar, the one that burned, and we were talking about painting and I asked you why you loved it so much."

"What did I say?"

"You looked off and said, like you didn't even know you were speaking, you said you could use paint to make a landscape, but no landscape could ever be a painting."

"And you understood that?"

"Not at all."

"That's a relief. I'm lucky you didn't sprint out of there. I have no fucking idea what I could have meant by that. You're sure that's what I said?"

Linda laughed softly. "I just fell in love with you again."

"You are a romantic," I told her.

"When did you fall in love with me?" she asked.

"The very first time I saw you."

"No, really."

"Really."

I was lying. I wanted to have fallen in love the way I had described. I wanted to fall again. We didn't make love. We were too exhausted from a day with the children, but we sat there on the porch deep into the night. The fireflies disappeared, the clouds drifted away and exposed the moon, then came back.

A light rain fell.

Back then Richard was married to a rather beautiful woman named Rachel. Rachel had been one of Richard's graduate students, but she quit her studies in order to pursue her relationship with her teacher, a move for which she blamed Richard, though he told a slightly and predictably different story. Nonetheless or nevertheless, who knows which is correct, they married, resentment not only intact but growing. Richard and Rachel rented a house in Edgartown during the same month that we were on the island. They needed to be able to walk to coffee and bagels, Richard said.

I met Richard for one of those bagels and a cup of coffee one Sunday morning. He'd asked me to join him at a place near the ferry dock.

"It's too hot to walk," Richard said.

"Then you'll be sitting here for a while," I said. "It's supposed to stay hot all week."

He nodded, pointed with his chin to something behind me. I paid him no mind. He was always trying to get me to notice attractive women.

I drank hot tea, believing it would make me cooler. I believed this because I had read it when I was a child and I believed it even though I had never had any experience of its actually working.

"Do you think I'm sexy?" Richard asked.

"I've only just met you," I said.

"No, really."

"Sexy?"

"Yeah, you know, sexy, alluring, seductive, desirable."

I added, "Sultry, slinky, toothsome. Do you mean beddable?" I glanced around to see if anyone was overhearing our talk. "I have to say, not to me, no."

"Imagine you were a woman."

"What's one thing have to do with the other?" I asked. "If I were a woman I still wouldn't find you sexy because I would no doubt be a lesbian. What's this all about anyway?"

"I think Rachel is tired of me."

"I can see why," I said.

"Physically, I mean."

"Where is all of this coming from? You don't sound like you."

"I don't know. It's probably because her best friend Barbara showed up and now it's like I'm not even here." He pushed his bagel across his plate. "They're like emotional Siamese twins or something. It's bad enough that they talk every day, but now that they're here together—" He picked up the bagel and tore off a bite. "Well, they're regular Papin sisters."

"You know, I don't pretend to get your obscure references, but I understand you now."

"You do?"

"You're a big baby who feels left out."

"Well, when you put it that way? So, you don't think they're at the house right now eating pussy?"

A woman at a near table looked up from her book.

"Keep your voice down," I said. "Let's look on the floor and see if we can't find your Y chromosome."

"You know what it is. She's too young for me."

"You mean, you're too old for her."

Richard nodded. "Who knew I'd be the one feeling insecure?"

"That would be everybody."

Needless to say, that marriage didn't last. To be fair, it lasted longer than I thought it would and ended without the explosion I had predicted, more of a fizzle. Luckily, neither Richard nor Rachel was terribly crushed, mostly exhausted and, I imagine, relieved.

"You made it past a year," I said. I held my glass of bourbon up to toast.

He touched his glass to mine. "I should have listened to you."

"I never said anything, did I?"

"But you thought it."

"Yes, I thought it."

"April's almost a teenager now. What's that like?"

"You're not allowed to marry my daughter," I said. "She's too old for you."

"She's cute, though." He poured more booze into our glasses. "And William, is he surviving the hormone storm?"

"I suppose. He's a little like me."

"Oblivious?"

"Exactly."

"Do you think he might want to go sailing with me tomorrow?"

"I think he'd love it."

"Kevin, why do you think I make bad choices?"

"Do you?"

"Like marrying Rachel."

I looked out his window at the dying lawn. "Rachel is a smart, beautiful woman. I would hardly call her a bad choice. It didn't work out."

"She's a lesbian."

"Well, she discovered that or finally admitted it to herself, however that works, but if she didn't know, how could you? Imagine how painful that was for her, hiding it, denying it."

"You're such a fucking good liberal. You're very reasonable when we talk about my life, aren't you?" Richard said. "Have you noticed that?"

I looked at him. "You've been talking to Linda."

"She says you work too much."

I nodded.

"She says you're drinking a lot."

I nodded again. "That might be true."

"Well, stop it."

The drinking too much was quiet in its way and yet, without causing physical disturbance, was violent enough. I would start around midday, innocuously, with a glass of wine and graduate pre-dinner to scotch or bourbon. It was a problem I didn't know I had until I was nearing the bottom of a bottle and so to avoid that feeling I would buy several bottles at once. The new complexion-challenged boy at the corner liquor store asked if I was having a party. I got into my car and started crying. But I didn't stop drinking. Instead I spread my purchases over a wider area, knowing the while how pathetic I was.

Paris

What I didn't tell you is that this music started with five measures of rests. What marks the beginning of the first measure? The poem has a woman and a man walking through a bare, cold wood. They are looking up at the moon set into a cloudless black sky. But then, but then after the wind presses against the man's back, we *O sieh, wie klar das Weltall schimmert! Es ist ein Glanz um Alles her.*

Victoire and I were to meet for lunch at La Contrescarpe in the fifth arrondissement and so we did meet there. I arrived first, as I arrive everywhere first; I am always early, a combination of poor planning and a desire to delude myself into thinking that I can have some control of a situation even if it is only that I get to see the world first. I sat in the café, surrounded by books that were mere decoration. Little ambience was achieved by the hodgepodge of titles, but the place was in truth memorable for its ornamentation. I found the farrago of spines more unsettling than anything else. It was a crisp, almost cold day. I sat with an espresso and watched people walk by, waited for one of them to be Victoire.

Seeing Victoire bounce toward me on rue Lacépède made me feel both young and old. She spotted me and smiled and for a moment I saw nothing but her youth and that left me feeling both bad and wonderful. She smiled at me and the bad feeling went away. I stood and pulled out a chair for her.

The waiter came over and Victoire ordered a coffee. She looked at me and, as if we had been in conversation for minutes, said, "Tell me something clever about painting."

I shook my head. "Wrong tree," I said.

"What does that mean?"

"It's an expression. 'You're barking up the wrong tree' means you're looking for answers in the wrong place."

"Then tell me something about painting. Anything."

"I can tell you about my eyes," I said.

"About your eyes?"

The waiter delivered Victoire's coffee.

"I hate my eyes. I have two of them and exactly the same thing goes into each."

"So, one of your eyes wants something different," she said. Her flirtation bothered me only because it made it apparent that she was smarter than I was.

"Do you live near here?" I asked.

"Very close." She sipped her coffee. "Where is your wife?"

"She's on a train. She arrives at four."

She looked around the café, lingered on the books. "I have never liked this place. Do you like it?"

"It's okay. Is there someplace you would rather go?"

"Yes. It is very close."

Very close was of course Victoire's flat. She was after all a water-colorist and her apartment was full of them. Thankfully they were not portraits of cows, but there was a preponderance of empty parks and stark river scenes. There was a large window that over-looked a garden. In the middle of the garden was a broken birdbath and I felt a little guilty when I realized I was paying more attention to it than to the many works of art. I turned my attention to her work and found them well done, but ordinary. I paused at a picture of a stream.

"This reminds me of Monet's *Ice Floes*."

"*Merci, monsieur*," she said and feigned a curtsy. "Would you like a glass of water?"

"Please."

She went to the small kitchen area and returned with one glass. She stood close to me while I took a sip, close enough that she made me nervous and somewhat charged. She bounced on the balls of her feet. I noticed this as I noticed that her feet were now bare. "This is where you try to kiss me and I turn away coyly."

I put my glass down and less awkwardly than I thought possible I placed my left hand around the young woman and pressed my fingers against the small of her back. She felt light and alive and I kissed her lips, softly, for several seconds and she did not pull away, coyly or otherwise, and I knew that I would never convincingly lie to myself that it felt anything but wonderful.

"Well, that was very nice," I said. "And now I must be going."

"What?"

"I'm sorry," I said, but I didn't let her go. "I'm no good at this." I knew I was lying. Apparently, I was quite good at this and my attempt at self-delusion was part of my less than clumsy flirtation. I kissed her again, and again she kissed me back. For so many years I had been with no one other than my wife, but my only clumsiness came during the few seconds that I considered that fact. Victoire was thin and broad shouldered and had a pronounced rib cage that pressed into me as I held her. She sighed but it was performance. I compared her to no one as I held her, as I continued to kiss her, as I raked my finger down her neck, her clavicle, and across a nipple beneath her thin sweater. She hardly had breasts and when she stepped back and removed her sweater with one fluid motion I could see just how beautiful her flat chest was. She dropped her sweater to the floor and looked away, said something about suddenly feeling shy. I remember clearly what I said to her, was happy to say it because finally I exercised some control in this play. I said, "Please don't let flirtation ruin our sex." She was taken by surprise and, I believe, aroused by my utterance. Even in the moment I was proud to have said *sex* instead of *lovemaking*. She came back to me, kissed me again, her mouth more open this time. I placed my hand behind her head, my fingers in her hair, and I pulled her back to look at her face. "Where is your bathroom?" I asked.

I did need to urinate, but what I really wanted was a break. In French fashion there was nothing in the toilet, but the toilet. There was no mirror and so I could not look at my face. Had I been able to stare myself down I might have made a quick decision to leave that little apartment. As I stared at the door, which offered no reflection, preparing to reenter the world, I could still feel Victoire's tongue just inside my mouth. It felt good to want this woman and I felt no guilt.

And yet I did not touch her again. I looked at her youthful hands, her neck, and reached for my coat.

"You're not leaving?"

"I think I should be."

"Stay longer."

"I have to meet my wife at her train." I said it so matter-of-factly that I startled myself.

"How old are your children?" she asked. She pulled the sheet over her lap.

"They're young. Six and two. April and Will."

"Are they as cute as I am?"

"In a different way."

"I should hope so."

I laughed as I tied my shoes. "How did you get to be this way?"

"What way is that?"

"Clever."

"It comes naturally. So much comes naturally."

"I'm sure."

"You're very brave," she said.

I looked at her, perhaps tilting my head like a confused dog. "Brave? What does being brave have to do with this?"

"Look at where you are. You're in the flat of a young French girl."

"That's not courage, that's weakness, lust, indulgence."

"Have it your way."

I looked at my watch.

"Will you come back?"

"I don't know." I looked at her face. I did want to see her again and so I nodded.

She turned to her desk and wrote down her phone number. "You can call me any time you like."

"I will do that."

Linda struggled with her bag down the platform. I pushed my way upstream through the disembarking passengers to get to her. I took the bag that hung from her shoulder and she held on to her rolling suitcase.

"Well, we're on time," she said. "That was some long train ride. How was your lunch?"

"Nice."

"Where did you eat?"

I told my first lie. "Of all places, the restaurant in Le Bon Marché."

"Did you buy me anything?"

"Sorry."

"I'm starving. Mind sitting with me while I eat?"

"Of course. Where do you want to go?"

"The bistro near the hotel is fine."

We walked from the station over to rue Saint-Placide where we sat outside under a heat lamp in a café right by the metro. Linda ordered a burger, fries, and a Coke. I ordered coffee.

"So, Bordeaux was not so good?"

"Not so *bon*. A big mall." She sipped her Coke. "Margaret seems to like it. I think it's probably better to live there than to visit."

"What's her husband like?"

Linda rolled her eyes. "Unemployed Italian guy. Leonardo. Didn't like him. Didn't trust him. He had a playboy vibe."

"Margaret must see something in him," I said.

"So what was it like with your young friend?"

I could have taken her question as an accusation, but it wasn't. "Enlightening."

"How so?"

"Talking to her, I wondered if I was ever that young. I must have been, but I can't remember it."

Linda's food arrived. "That was quick. *Merci*."

"Etienne asked me to stay on another two weeks," I told her. My French agent had mentioned my remaining in Paris a while longer, but had only suggested it in passing. "There are some buyers he wants me to meet."

"Of course. You should stay. Are you sure you're not staying for your new girlfriend?" Linda smiled at me, her joking smile.

I didn't respond to that.

House

I suppose every alcoholic desires to regard himself as simply a harmless drunk, wants to believe that no one really sees him for what he is. No, I never flew into rages or stumbled late and noisily into dance recitals or yelled a little too loud and made inappropriate comments at soccer games, but I became acutely aware that I wore a sickly sweet late-evening cologne and I noticed how my children looked at my eyes, holding them for too long and looking away too quickly. But mostly I was made ashamed by the way Linda turned away from me every night, her pretend-sleeping face aimed at the window. I could tell from the attitude of the back of her head that she was wide awake and stressed out, it being in her breathing, how stiff and close her elbows were held to her frame. There was no one reason that triggered my cold turkey suspension, and I use *suspension* here as a nod to that common and perhaps correct thinking, that one can all too easily fall prey to the bottle at any time. Truth be told, I didn't miss the bottle when I decided to stop and I don't miss it now. There was no poignant comment from a wise child, no epiphany at all worth mentioning, just a slow growing sick of myself. I had to stop cold turkey and I had a catalyst. I was never any good in groups. There was just too much God in AA and that might have driven me to drink and drugs. What I found to sustain my effort was my private painting, which ironically seemed to be as damaging to my family as cognac. It was certainly materially more expensive; paint is pricey stuff. The painting did both bring me back to my family and drive a formidable wedge between us. I only occasionally worked into the wee hours the way I claimed to work when I was a mere drunk. I cannot say that I was more attentive to the workings of my family, though I was physically more present, but my mind was nearly always on the painting or in the painting or around the painting. It was far more socially acceptable to be a workaholic, the obsessed artiste, than it was to be a drunk, but, using an old neighbor's phrase, *I'm here to tell you* that one addiction was as bad as the next.

The real sadness was that I drifted away from my wife and children because of alcohol, but instead of finding the current back to them when I ceased, I camped out on an uncharted island in the middle of myself. Nonetheless, selfish as I was, things were better. I was more trustworthy. An absentminded artist is more forgivable than an alcoholic.

A few people didn't, couldn't, or wouldn't believe that I had stopped cold turkey. How did you do it? they would ask. My answer was simple, completely honest, and unsatisfactory. By not drinking anymore, I would say. A true lie.

When interviewers came to ask me questions I would become a little cranky and a little disappointed in myself for my brand of vanity. I voiced complaint that they were taking up my time, but was simultaneously pleased by their attention. I would retreat, become oddly literal, understandably I thought, anti-jargon, even anti-intellectual, slipping into some deeply held, perhaps self-conscious, probably a bit disingenuous, certainly indulgent way of thinking that art could only derive from a place of innocence, naïveté, if that was not a contradiction, of pure mind. One nice enough woman from *Artforum*, an amply smart person, with almost a lisp, inquired about the use of letter stenciling in some of my early paintings.

"Why did you always use the same typeface in the stenciling? What does that style of letter mean to you?" she asked.

"I used those stencils because those were the stencils they had at the hardware store."

"But that particular typeface in all of them, why?"

"That's the way the stencils came."

"But if you had wanted a different look, would you have been averse to cutting your own stencils?"

"Why would I do that? They had them at the hardware store."

"Then you like these the best," she said.

"Yes."

"But why?" she wanted to know.

"Because that is the way they came."

"Do you use these stencils because you like them or simply be-cause that is the way they come?" She was becoming annoyed, I thought.

"That is what I like about them. I like them because they came that way."

1979

"Or what?" I asked once we were back in the Caddy. "Be on time or what? He's going to leave without us?"

"I take it you don't like him," Richard said.

"He's a fucking asshole. I don't know if you noticed that. We can't actually go out into the countryside with this racist idiot."

"I think he can help me find my brother."

I said nothing. Of course Richard was right; I also believed the asshole would be able to find Tad. I did not tell Richard that I was not convinced that his brother was worth finding.

We drove the congested streets forty minutes back to the hotel, where he parked the Caddy right in front. He checked in, tossed our bags into the corners, and we lay on our backs on the same bed and stared up at the nonfunctioning ceiling fan. I imagined the tick it might have made if it worked.

"I think it just moved," Richard said.

"Nope. If it had moved I would have felt it. I didn't feel anything, so it didn't move."

"It moved a millimeter."

"I would have felt it."

"We should go out and find some food," Richard said.

"I'm too hot to eat."

"It's not hotter than where we came from."

"It feels hotter."

"Maybe we should go out and get drunk."

"No, I don't think that's wise. We've got to get up at six so we can meet Custer at seven. I don't want a hangover when I'm dealing with a homicidal maniac. To say the least, I don't trust him. Hell, I'm afraid of him. He might drive us thirty miles out of town, shoot us, and take the money."

"I hadn't thought of that." Richard sighed. "I won't take the money. I'll tell him he'll get it when I get my brother."

"Listen to us. This is one fucked-up situation. You read fucking Old English. I'm a fucking painter."

"Sorry."

I felt suddenly like shit. "Hey, you're my best friend. I'm here because I want to be. Okay?"

"Thanks," Richard said. "I know this is some shit."

"But you're right though. We really need go out there and find something to eat. If we are going out with Attila the idiot in the morning, then we had better have some strength."

We dragged ourselves down the stairs, out and down the street to a small fish stew restaurant where we ate undercooked bread, black beans and rice, and fish stew. Richard drank a beer.

"At least the food is good," I said.

"I thought a Cadillac was supposed to have a smooth ride," Richard said.

"That would be on a smooth road. A paved road."

Richard tore a tortilla in half.

"Richard, are you sure you want your brother back?"

He stared at me.

"I didn't mean it like that. But what are we really doing here? Are we saving him?"

Richard drank from his bottle of beer.

"Forget that I said anything."

"Kevin, he's my brother."

"I know."

"You really don't have to come tomorrow. I'd understand."

"But I am here, aren't I?" I raised my water glass in a toast. "To finding your brother."

He waited a beat then tapped my glass with his beer bottle. "Thank you."

As we lay in bed that night, I couldn't sleep. I thought that was a reasonable enough response to the situation. Richard slept fitfully, also a reasonable response. The voices outside on the street never ceased. Music played from a bar somewhere. I looked for at least one voice inside my head that might talk me out of continuing with this insane business. I suppose the mere search for such a voice actually constituted one, but it was either too faint or too unpersuasive, or I simply wasn't listening. Regardless, I did have the thought that the sheets might as well have been soaked with blood instead of our sweat. I was in this now.

I must have slept for at least a few minutes because my brain decided to dream. I assumed it was a dream, but it may well have been one of those internal voices that I so wanted to hear. I woke up disturbed, but unable to recall the events of the dream. If I had remembered the dream it would probably have involved slow drowning, certainly not flying, and there would have been a little three-legged whiskey-colored dog in it. But that's only if I could have dredged it up. The feeling left with me when I did awake, when I did open my eyes to stare at the unmoving faded wood fan blades, was that I was as much immersed in a dream as ever.

The sun came up when no one was looking. We woke up buzzed, anxious, anything but happy and eager. We decided not to shower after I suggested that it seemed pointless to enter a bloodbath with clean underwear.

"Are you going to ask me some stupid question like *are you ready*?" I tied my second boot.

"Nope."

"Good."

"At least it's a little cooler," Richard said.

I nodded, walked across the room, and looked down at the empty street. "For a while anyway."

We left the hotel room, walked down the stairs and through the deserted lobby. On the hood of the Caddy we found a pile of dog shit.

"Tall dog," Richard said.

I grabbed some newspaper out of the gutter and knocked the shit off the car. "Do you get the feeling we're not welcome here?"

The boat's engine hesitated and then turned over, startled the neighborhood dogs. We drove away. I cracked open an orange and we shared it on the way.

"Scared?" Richard asked.

"Too stupid to be scared. Really, what's the worst thing that could happen? He shoots us and stabs us and chops off our heads. That doesn't scare me. We live on Baltimore Avenue in Philadelphia."

Richard nodded. "Good point."

A beautiful woman crossed the street in front of us. Her dress was pastel pink, almost white.

"She's off to work," I said. "What do you think she does?"

"No uniform. No briefcase. I think she works in a bank. What do you think?"

"Hotel maybe."

"Okay," Richard said.

"Am I scared?" I repeated his question and looked over at him. "Are you fucking kidding me? I've already shit my pants."

"So, are you going to marry Linda?"

"Who the fuck knows? I'm not ready to marry anybody. And would she want to marry me?"

"Well, there's that."

The door of the Bummer's trailer was propped open with a broken cinder block when we arrived. The one-man army was dressed in the same T-shirt he was wearing the day before or at least one exactly like it. He stood leaning in the jamb holding a battered metal ice chest.

"Good morning, ladies," he said. His smile appeared almost genuine.

We stepped toward him.

The Bummer stepped down and put the chest on the ground. "Put this in the backseat. And be fucking careful with it."

That made me nervous.

"What's in there?" Richard asked.

"What do you think is in there?" Before Richard and I could say anything or think to say anything, he said, "It's beer. Just beer. Gotta have beer. Just put the chest on the backseat."

I picked up the chest.

"Boom!" the Bummer shouted.

I dropped the chest and hopped backward.

The Bummer laughed. He pulled open the lid of the chest. "Beer." He slammed the lid down. "What did you think was in there? Explosives? Guns?" He turned and walked back into the trailer.

I picked up the chest.

Richard looked at me and shrugged. The situation was not getting any sweeter.

It became even less sweet when Sergeant Caligari reemerged from the trailer holding an M16 and what looked like a .45-caliber pistol in a shoulder holster. "Here are the guns," he said. He paused to enjoy the looks on our faces. "These are *my* fuckin' guns. Don't touch them. Those are *my* beers. Don't touch them. Y'all understand?" He lit a cigarette, laughed, and then pointed northeast toward the hills. "We're going up there."

"And you need guns?" I asked.

"Oh, yeah. Always need guns." The Bummer walked to the Caddy and pushed his rifle through the window into the backseat. He opened the passenger-side door and pushed forward the front seat. "There's a war going on in this country, boys." He climbed into the rear. "Put that chest right here beside me."

I did.

Standing at the open driver's-side door, Richard said, "I want to know where we're going."

"I told you, girlfriend. We're headed for them thar hills."

Richard and I got into the car. Richard cranked the engine and steered us onto the rutted road.

"Enjoy this good road while it lasts," the Bummer said. "While you boys were snoozing or whatever you do at night, I was already hard at work. Heard me a rumor about a gringo looking for coke up near the volcano."

"Somebody just shoved a handwritten note under your door in the middle of the night," I said.

"Pretty much."

The pop of a beer can being opened made me jump. I glanced back at the Bummer.

"Don't worry, boy, we ain't in Mississippi. It's hot like Mississippi, but it ain't Mississippi." He lounged with the M16 across his lap. The rifle scared me. He scared me.

A skinny, rib-showing dog took his time crossing the road in front of us and Richard slowed the car.

"Run that motherfucker over," the Bummer said.

Richard did not do that.

"Ricky, you're going to come to a fork in the road up here. Veer left." The Bummer closed his eyes and seemed to drift into sleep, a beer can in his left hand, the right draped over the gun.

Richard and I didn't speak. We veered left onto an even rougher dirt road. The big car bottomed out more than a few times. We looked out at the land. We moved from brown to green, from low to high.

Finally, I broke the silence. "I like green."

"What?" Richard said.

"The color green. I like it. I don't use it much. Can't control it. The Mona Lisa is wearing green and so you know she's not nobility."

"Is that right."

"In Chinese, blue and green are the same word."

"In Vietnam, too," the Bummer said from behind us. "Confused the shit out of me until I figured it out. Look at the green sky." He closed his eyes again. "Drive until you can't drive."

Richard mouthed the words "I'm sorry."

As we continued up I noticed clouds collecting just to the east, huge cottony clouds that were flat on the bottom as if they were sitting on a glass table. The trees changed from live oak and dogwood to pine and cedar. The road became more twisted until I lost all notion of east, west, north, and south and it became not only rougher, bumpier, but also more treacherous, narrow, narrow enough on some turns to create doubt as to whether our boat of a car would fit.

"Those clouds look bad," I said.

"That's all we need, for this road to get wet." Just as Richard finished his sentence huge raindrops hit the windshield. Then it was raining.

"Stop the car," the Bummer said. I hadn't known he was awake. It bothered me that he was awake.

Richard skidded the car to a rest.

"Out," the Bummer said.

"Are we here?" Richard asked.

"Just get out."

Richard got out. So did I. The rain was falling hard.

"Open the trunk," the Bummer said as he pulled himself out of the car.

Richard tossed me a panicked look over the hood.

"Why do you want me to open the trunk?"

The Bummer reached back into the car and took the keys from the ignition. He walked to the back of the car. I was encouraged by the fact that he had left the M16 in the backseat, though he still wore the holstered pistol. "Rocks!" he shouted as he opened the trunk. "Big ones."

We stood there.

"Listen, my pretty motherfuckers, if we don't weigh down the back of this beast she'll fishtail all over the fuckin' place and we'll end up down there." He pointed over the cliff.

I looked down and I felt as if I was seeing the drop-off for the first time. From Richard's expression I could see the same was true for him. We found large rocks and loaded them, the rain beating down on us the while. It stopped just as I slammed shut the lid.

The Bummer fell into the backseat again. "Well, let's get going."

Even with the much-needed weight in the rear, the Caddy still swung wildly on the fresh mud in the very next curve.

"I understand it now," Richard said. "Got to brake before the curve. Before the curve."

"Sounds right," I said. I looked into the backseat. The Bummer seemed again to be sleeping.

"He asleep?" Richard asked.

"Who knows."

The sun came out, but the road remained wet. We came to a stretch of road that straightened out under a canopy of trees.

"Are those monkeys?" Richard asked.

There were spider monkeys, dozens of them, swinging through the branches above us.

"Toto," I said.

"Don't say it," Richard said.

For some reason, as we rolled along under that strange awning of limbs and chattering primates, I thought of the paintings that had been haunting me. Not only my own, but those of others, my influences, mainly expressionists, but also the cubists. I recalled Kafka's complaint about some poem, saying that it was just so much screaming and that was where I thought I had landed. It was a wretched place to be at such a young age. I of course had plenty to scream about and yet nothing at all. I didn't deserve my screams and yet there were my paintings, boisterous, strident, stormy maybe, rough, angry, and, finally, undisciplined and arrogant. And so, quite in keeping with my self-indulgence, I began to slip into my familiar pit of self-loathing. I realized how tired, how afraid I was.

"What is it?" Richard asked.

"Nothing," I said, it being both true and false. "These monkeys make me think of Rousseau."

"Painter or philosopher?"

"Very funny."

We drove on for an hour.

We crested a hill and there was a gentle slope in front of us, the road lightly wending through ocher grass. The colors brought me around. A cantina sat at the side of the road ahead of us.

The air rushing through the car was considerably colder now. I rubbed my arms as I didn't have a jacket.

A beer popped open in the backseat. "You're going to want to stop here," the Bummer said.

House

A painting has many surfaces. To say that a painting is like a story is a pedestrian utterance, not altogether untrue, but uninspired, though that hardly stops people from making such invidious and unwarranted comparisons. The painting that was my life was static, hardly a story at all, moving but with no moving parts, changing but without alteration. The shapes in the painting were unique elements in unique situations, I knew that, but I never pressed that thinking beyond my canvas. The shapes were organisms with volition and a desire for self-assertion. But the shapes could push back and every shape possessed a color.

Every bowl of cereal I ever poured was the same color but no bowl was ever the same. That might or might not be a true thing about colors. Or perhaps about bowls of cereal. Regardless, Heraclitus, I had poured a bowl of sugary cereal for my sixteen-year-old daughter. Her name is April and though I loved and love her very much I never liked her name or the month.

April was beautiful because she was my daughter, but being an artist and being able to step outside myself to see, I saw that she might be seen as plain, though I liked that look, thought it more interesting than the word *plain*. She had been ignoring me all morning, but when her brother made his exit from the kitchen she actually looked at me. As startled as I was by this simple connection, I was not surprised by her telling me that we needed to talk. Linda was out at her Pilates class and so we were alone.

I sat at the table with her. I felt awkward. Truth was I would have felt awkward if I hadn't felt awkward. "Okay, what are we talking about?"

"You know how you have that painting out there? At least we think there's a painting in there."

"Yes."

"It's a secret, right?"

"I guess. I hadn't thought about it like that."

"But it's your private thing, right?"

"That's true."

"You don't want anyone else to see it."

"That's true enough." I got up to pour myself a cup of coffee, but more I was trying to break her control over the conversation. "So, what is this all about?" I sat back down.

"I have a secret."

"Okay."

"You have to promise not to tell Mom," she said.

"Well, I can't say I can do that."

"I won't tell you unless you promise." She paused to listen for movement in the rest of the house. "Promise me."

"Okay, I promise."

"You won't tell her."

"Okay."

"I'm pregnant," she said.

I surprised myself by remaining very calm. I blew on my coffee and watched her eyes until she looked away. "Are you all right?" I asked.

"I'm pregnant," she said, as if I were being thick-headed and not understanding her.

"I heard you and I want to know if you're all right."

"Aren't you mad?"

"I don't know enough to be mad. I just want you to be all right. No, I'm not mad at you."

"You're disappointed."

"Are you all right?" I asked again.

"I think so. Don't you want to know who the father is?" April was tearing up now, yet her voice did not break.

"Is that really important? I'm concerned about you."

"You can't tell Mom," she said, regaining composure.

"Well, that's going to be difficult."

"You promised."

She was right, I had promised. My quiet manner had always been a failing and it was now as well, my wanting but being unwilling to ask or incapable of asking the questions that I imagined an outraged parent should ask. But I wasn't outraged, not angry, not disappointed, not terribly upset. I was only concerned and in a way, even at that precise moment, I was a bit proud of myself. And as quickly I felt shame for at all considering myself at that moment.

"You promised," she repeated.

I nodded. I had made a promise, in no uncertain terms. I wondered just what I had done. Was it an admission to an obligation to remain silent or merely a prediction that I would not? Richard had promised me that he would destroy my painting should I die of a sudden, but neither of us was deluded enough not to imagine that he would likely be unable to follow through. But how could I fail in this promise? It occurred to me that whereas my promise was voluntary, more or less, my obligation to abide by it was anything but. It was rather straightforward and for some reason it felt more binding for the fact that I was pressed into making it; it was not my idea. I looked at my daughter's face. She was so young. How could she be pregnant? "You know," I said, "this is not the sort of thing you can hide indefinitely."

"I won't have to," she said.

I was a clumsy old father, but I wasn't completely clueless. "You're certain about this?" I asked.

"I'm sixteen years old, Dad. I can't have a baby."

"All right."

"Do you have a problem with me having an abortion?"

"I don't know. I've never thought about it. I haven't had a chance to think about it. I mean no, I don't have a problem with it. I have a problem with your mother not knowing about this."

"In case you haven't noticed, Mom and I haven't been getting along all that well lately."

That came as news to me. I had known for some time that I was out of the family loop, but I didn't know how much. And now I didn't know whether I was being manipulated by my daughter and if so, to what end. Whatever the case, I felt guilty for having been so distracted, so self-absorbed, most sadly maybe self-intrigued, that I was ignorant, oblivious about the dynamics of my family. I didn't know enough to know whether it was true that she and her mother were estranged.

"Why aren't you two getting along?" I asked.

April shrugged. "It's a mother-daughter thing."

"What about us? Do we get along?"

"It depends on what you mean by get along. We don't fight. We also don't talk. We don't know what's going on with each other. I don't think you've asked me one question in over a year."

"Is that true?"

April shrugged, smiled. "That you don't know is an answer of sorts, don't you think?"

"I guess it is. I'm sorry."

The thing I admired about Leonardo da Vinci was his insatiable hunger to understand everything around him. A good thing in an artist, but at this I was a miserable failure, wanting at every turn to know how light affected color, how texture affected spatial orientation, and yet, in regard to my own inner life, I was oblivious as to how my secrets had influenced, shaped my vision, in the most literal sense. But unlike my hero Leonardo's beautiful method of extracting nature's secrets from painstaking observation, I had deluded myself into believing that nature would simply reveal itself to me, like the coral of a sunset, like the many whites of snow. Instead, I failed even to see the most transparent and patent features of my own family. I was ashamed of myself.

"And so what do I do?" I asked Richard. We were sitting in the pleasant little coffee shop not far from the university campus. "Do I actually keep this thing to myself?"

"This is why I never had children." Richard looked out the window at a couple of passing students. "They let them in younger every year. Were we ever so young?"

I watched Richard sip his too-sweet iced coffee drink through a straw. "Do you know what you look like drinking that?"

"A sophisticate?"

I said nothing.

"You made a promise," Richard said.

"Sort of."

"Did you say 'I promise'?"

I looked out the window.

"Then there is no *sort of*. A promise is a magic incantation that changes you and the world around you. Hume compared it to transubstantiation."

"Yeah, well, he wasn't serious."

"Still."

"There is no way I can keep this from Linda."

"I agree," Richard said.

"So you believe it's okay for me to break my promise?"

"I didn't say that. It's never okay to break a promise. A promise is a promise is a promise. Then there's the whole secret thing."

"Secret thing?"

"Your daughter, the teenage girl you thought didn't know you existed or at least she didn't care in the least, chose you of all people to keep the biggest secret of her life up to this point."

"We know a little about secrets, don't we?"

"Do you know who the father is?"

"No."

"Did you ask?"

"I don't care," I told him, looked into my empty coffee cup.

Richard was mute for a beat, playing with his straw. "You know, you might want to ask her that. How does she know she's really pregnant? Did she take a test or just miss her period?"

"I was a little stunned when she told me. I didn't want to turn the moment into an interrogation. I should have her see the doctor."

"What about the father? What if the father wants the baby? Doesn't he have rights?"

"Fuck the father. I don't care who he is or what his rights are. I care about my daughter. I care about April."

"If I still smoked I'd light a cigarette right now," Richard said. "I imagine that marriage is a kind of promise, a promise to share everything or some shit like that. So, you've got two promises to keep and keeping either one means breaking the other. You're what we call *fucked*."

"You're very helpful."

"Of course you have to tell Linda," he said.

"I know that."

The young waitress came and I sent her away. I watched her collect an order from the counter. Her hands were olive, smooth, young. I wondered what secrets she had told her father.

"I know I have to tell Linda," I said. "I have to tell her because it's the right thing to do."

"Yeah."

"And I have to tell her because I need her help in this. I'm not certain how to best help April."

1979

The cantina was so much a cliché that it wasn't one. It was a small cinder-block affair with a short door roughly constructed out of two-by-sixes and two-by-fours. The Bummer carried his half-drunk beer as we entered, he being rather loud upon doing so, singing "Yankee Doodle," of all tunes. The floor was dirt, but, perhaps from being covered for so long, was not the same dirt as outside, it being darker yet less red, a little finer. There were two booths, two tables, four stools at a battered strangely waist-high bar. A fat woman tended a sloppily made fireplace in the corner of the far wall. The room was smoky and thick with the almost pleasant smell of burning wood. There was a bearded man behind the bar and another man seated in a booth, his face down on folded arms on the table.

"Give me that picture," the Bummer said. He turned to look at Richard. "Give me that picture of your brother."

Richard gave it to him.

"You two go and have a seat over there," the Bummer said. "In the pretty green booth."

We did as instructed. We watched as the psycho walked cockily up to the bar; he walked like John Wayne, a near limp, almost a stagger.

"*Hola, amigo,*" he said. "*Cómo estás?*"

The bartender said nothing as he drew near.

The Bummer held the photo up for the man to see, looked at it himself. "*Has visto a este hombre?*"

"I no see this man," the bartender said in English.

"Has Carlos been around?"

The man shook his head.

The Bummer stared at him for a couple of seconds then called to the woman. *"Yo, mamacita!"*

The woman glanced up for a second, then turned back to the fire, shaking her head.

The Bummer walked away, laughed noiselessly, and then walked over to the sleeping drunk. He grabbed the man by his hair and lifted his head, looked at his face, and let it fall back to the table with a thud.

Richard caught my eyes and said, "What the fuck?"

I shrugged.

The Bummer came to our booth, but didn't sit. He looked at the ceiling and around the tavern. "I got what I came for."

"And what's that?" I asked.

"You didn't learn anything," Richard said. "You showed them the picture and you didn't learn a fucking thing."

"Maybe, maybe not. Now let's blow this pop stand."

I felt like an idiot following that asshole back out to the Caddy, but what else could we do now?

"So, what now?" Richard asked.

"We drive on. There's something I want to look at."

"And what's that?" I asked.

"Collecting intel."

"Intel," I said, looking at Richard and probably rolling my eyes.

"I thought you said we were going about thirty miles," Richard said. "This is way more than thirty miles."

"Misjudged."

We fell into the Caddy and drove on. We traveled deeper into the mountains, the road, fortunately, not quite as treacherous as before. A blue bus with a couple of passengers passed us going the other way and I realized we had not seen another vehicle all day.

"What's the story?" I said. "Why no cars on this road?" I looked into the backseat when there came no answer and saw that the Bummer was again asleep. "He's out again."

Richard just stared at the road. His was angry and perhaps a bit embarrassed that he'd gotten us into this.

"Pull over." This from the backseat. The Bummer was different now, more serious or nervous, skittish, I didn't know which but I found it mildly alarming. If not before, then certainly at that point things became dreamlike, not in the hazy, milky sort of dreamscape way, but in the sharply defined, intensely clarified, markedly illuminated dream, scarier than the other kind and so clear that it defied interpretation.

"You girls ready to get wet?" the Bummer asked.

"What?" From Richard.

"Stay behind me," the psycho said.

We did. We followed him across the road to a dirt lane that I had not noticed, far too rough for the Cadillac. After about a couple hundred meters the lane became a trail. We climbed.

"You boys believe in God?" the Bummer asked. He slung the rifle over his shoulder.

"No," I said. "Do you?"

"I was raised to believe in God," the Bummer said.

"Do you?" I asked. "Actually believe in God?"

"Yeah, there's a god, but he's no good at his job. He's a fuckup. There's probably a family of them, gods, and we got the stupid one."

As we approached the crest of a hill, the Bummer motioned for us to stop, held a crooked index finger to his pursed lips. He dropped to all fours and crawled to the top and looked over. He rested his chin on his rifle. Richard and I dropped down and worked our way up to join him.

Below us there was nothing but an empty meadow of tall pea-green grass, the wind scratching the nap of it, changing the color from dark to light and back. The Bummer looked over at us and nodded, as if to say, "There you have it."

"What are we looking at?" I asked.

"Nothing," he said. "That's the point."

"What's the point?" I looked at Richard. He appeared sick, like he might vomit. "Why the fuck did you bring us out here?" I asked.

"How were we going to see that there's nothing here if we didn't fuckin' come here?"

I paused, somewhat stunned by his irreproachable logic, though dismayed by his dull-wittedness. "What does it mean that there's nothing here?"

"Why are you even talking to this son of a bitch?" Richard asked me. "The man is crazy."

"Who the fuck are you calling crazy?" The Bummer's tone shifted to menace and we were reminded, jarringly, that he was armed.

"Well, you are crazy," I said.

He glared at me the way he had during that first meeting in his trailer. Then his face softened. "I guess that's right." He smiled and stood up. "I guess everybody's a little crazy."

That was easily the craziest and most unhinged thing he had yet said, not because it was untrue but simply for the fact that it was being uttered by a crazy man. Sadly, I had to agree with him and was quite convinced that we were equally crazy for just being there.

"So, where to now?" Richard asked, a step behind the Bummer. "Where do we find our next nothing?"

The Bummer looked at the sky. "It gets dark fast up here. We can build a fire and sleep outside or we can sleep in the car or we can drive all the fucking way back to town just to drive back here tomorrow. What do you think?"

Richard and I kicked at the dirt. I think he didn't know what to say as much as I didn't know what to say. "It's cold out here," I said to end our somewhat ham-fisted silence.

"It's cold out here," the Bummer mocked me.

"We didn't come prepared to camp out," Richard said.

"Pussies," the Bummer said. "Come on. Drive us back to the cantina."

"Why?"

"We'll spend the night there," the Bummer said. "Nice warm fire. Great conversation."

"So, we're going all the way back there?" I said. "And where do
we go in the morning?"

"Why, we continue our search."

"Stop talking to him," Richard said. "Just stop talking to him."

After driving through a hum of awkward silence I stopped the car in
the same spot in front of the cantina.

The Bummer led us back into the tavern. *"Dormimos aqui,"* he an-
nounced to the bartender. *"Cerveza, por favor."*

The fire was still burning, but the old woman was gone. The
drunk remained, head on table. We fell clumsily into the same booth,
Richard and I across from the Bummer.

"Some beers, some sleep, and tomorrow we find your brother,"
the Bummer said, snapping his fingers to hurry the bartender.

"Fuck you," Richard said.

The Bummer didn't acknowledge him, but put a cigarette in his
mouth. "Tomorrow," he repeated.

The little man brought us the beers, put them on the table, and
just walked away. I thanked the man. The Bummer thanked him
louder.

The Bummer looked at us in turn and then took his beer and sat
opposite the drunk man in the other booth. He lay down on the seat.
I moved to occupy the bench across from Richard and lay down also,
closed my eyes. "We really ought to sleep," I sighed.

"It's hardly dark," Richard said.

"I don't care."

"He's asleep. We can just get in the car and go back to the city. Fly
home tomorrow."

"Not that I think that's a bad idea, but I don't trust us to find our
way, especially in the dark."

Richard did not argue.

It was still dark when I awoke from a rather uncomfortable, fitful
sleep made worse by a dream that had me dressed like a Vietnamese
farmer, conical straw hat and all, hiding in a rice paddy in the pitch
darkness waiting for American soldiers to pass by. As a Vietnamese

man I knew that one of the soldiers was the one they called the Bummer. The fear was a real feeling, intense, discordant, even if the dream was uneventful, even boring. I was awake before either Richard or the Bummer. The cantina had actually been shut down. The only light came from an oversized neon Budweiser sign that read *ud ser*. The fire was now mere embers. The bartender was gone, but the drunk still occupied the seat opposite the Bummer. I walked outside to pee and found that thick fog had rolled in, so dense that I could not see the Cadillac, which was a couple of yards away. I must have either drifted off to sleep standing there, dick in hand, or simply spaced out, because I snapped to and discovered that someone was standing next to me, urinating as well. It was the Bummer.

"I just love to piss," the Bummer said, slipping his feet to widen his stance. "You young fellas can have your sex, but I'll take a good long piss any day. Nothing like it. Am I right?"

"Right," I said. What does one say to talk like that? My parents taught me better than to antagonize homicidal maniacs. Sadly, they had not trained me well enough to avoid predicaments like this one.

"You and your buddy okay? This is going to get a little rougher, you know," the Bummer said. He shook off and zipped up. "No matter how much you wiggle and dance."

I looked at his face for a few seconds. "Can you really find his brother? Or are you just fucking with us?"

"I can find him," he said with the same rusty bravado he had used in his trailer.

I wanted to ask him what the useless drive out into the middle of nowhere was all about, but I didn't.

Richard stumbled out to join us. He peed while he yawned wide. "Are we there yet?"

"Just about," I said. "I guess we're closer. Bummer here tells me he really can find Tad."

"Righto," Richard said. "I was hoping all this fog meant that this was a fucking dream."

House

When I asked Linda to marry me she thought I was joking. She started laughing immediately and I have to say that it hurt my feelings. Then she caught the look on my face. Perhaps it was dismay or disappointment, maybe simply embarrassment, but she stopped laughing. I was at least not idiotic enough to attempt the proposal in a public place, out of aesthetic choice or timidity, I still don't know, but instead I asked her on the back porch of the house I shared with Richard on Baltimore Avenue in Philadelphia. Richard wasn't there. It was midafternoon and the neighbor's dog, a whippet, would not stop barking. She touched my face.

"Are you serious?" she asked.

"You've said more romantic things," I told her.

"Yes, Kevin Pace, I will marry you." She smiled and made me relax. "Who else would have you?"

"That's why I'm asking you."

We walked down the street to the little shop that sold nothing but carrot cakes, all kinds of carrot cakes. We bought her favorite, carob and raspberry, brought it back to the house, ate it all and drank wine while we sat in the bay window.

"Do you think we will have a good life together?" I asked.

"I wouldn't say yes if I thought otherwise." She sipped her wine and stared at me. "Are you all right?"

"You ask because I proposed?"

"No. I ask because ever since you came back from El Salvador you seem distant. Different. I don't know. Are you sad about something?"

"Just nervous," I lied. "I'm relieved you said yes."

"Are you now?"

"I didn't want to have to go to the next name on the list," I told her.

"Really now."

"I thought three deep was enough."

Linda smiled, touched my hand. "You're a lucky man. Are you sure you're okay? Did something happen down in El Salvador with Richard?"

"Nothing happened." I could not stomach the idea that she might think my proposal was tied to sadness, my failure. And as I didn't tell her then, I knew that I could not tell her, would not tell her ever. Whether my intended commitment to Linda, my newfound resolve, was in some way an act of self-preservative distancing or merely an attempt to make things feel normal I would never know, perhaps did not want to know. We lay together that night and I think she might have slept or she could have been pretending like me. When I was a kid I would pretend to fall asleep on car trips with my family and then I would pretend to dream. That night with Linda I pretended to dream a painting that would change our lives.

I made the canvas. It was a large canvas, eight by six feet. It was called *Two Yellows* and it had on it two yellows, corn yellow and icterine, very close, but importantly different. A review by a well-known critic said that I had made the happy colors somber, the bright hues subdued and unsmiling. It all seemed to be a good thing to the critic, but to me he seemed to be saying that the canvas was lugubrious, morose and joyless, which was true enough. I had not painted it with a sense of irony, but it was all so ironic. To me the yellows were two of those colors between green and orange, violet being the complement. Yellow in nature is the most visible color, easy to find, but perhaps, I imagined, not so easy to see.

Butterflies.

Paris

I could not go with Linda to her gate because of security and there were no restaurants outside the gates at Charles de Gaulle, so we sat on a bench just outside the terminal. Linda seemed to have second thoughts about my remaining in Paris.

"I'm going to miss you," she said.

"Me too. But you have work to get back to and it seems I have work here," I said. "I'll be here less than two weeks."

"Is that really why you're staying? Work?"

"What are you asking me?"

"Kevin, we've been married for a long time," she said.

"And?"

"You know."

"Nothing like that."

"Have you ever?" I asked.

She shook her head, but she was lying. I was surprised, but not hurt, nor was I encouraged or validated, the absence of these feelings, convenient rationalizations immediately evident to me. I didn't care, but realized that I wanted Linda to have her secrets. I wanted to let her off the hook.

"Do you remember *Two Yellows*?" I asked.

"Of course."

"It's just a painting," I told her. "The more it tells you the less you know. A lesson from nature."

She stared at me, rightly confused. "I'm afraid I don't know what you're talking about."

"It would help if I did," I said.

Time came for her to go. I watched her walk through passport control and then I took the RER back to Paris. The train was empty but for a tattooed girl who sat facing me, staring. Her left arm was a sleeve of tiger stripes. She had several rings in her lower lip, all on the right side.

The train kept moving and we just stared at each other. Then it occurred to me that she was American. I didn't know how I knew it, but I did. Her black vest over a T-shirt was in no way a giveaway. Her jeans were just jeans and her boots were like those I had seen many French young women wearing.

"You are American," I said.

She was stunned.

"So am I," I said. "Do those rings in your lip hurt?"

"Sometimes."

"Where are you from?"

"Portland, Oregon. What about you?"

"Rhode Island."

A load of young people noisily boarded the car at Gare du Nord. I watched Tiger Arm attend to them. "Don't worry," I said. "I won't tell."

I went to a café near the Odéon. I sat on the street and watched people as I waited for Victoire. I was eager to see her. I was interested in seeing her, a strange feeling, but the description was accurate. When I did spot her half a block away I felt relief. It wasn't that I considered at all that she would stand me up, but I simply felt set free by seeing her. It was a good feeling, a guilty feeling, a good feeling because of the guilt and it was a vanishing guilt because it felt so good. As she crossed the Boulevard Saint-Michel, catching me staring as she approached, she smiled, not the same flirtatious, kittenish smile she had used before, but a real smile and I felt, for lack of a better word, happy.

1979

The fog had not burned off an hour later when we took a turn off the same road we had traveled the previous day. I was driving and the Bummer was in the passenger seat, leaning forward, peering through the haze. His attitude was different again, even more serious, nervous, pensive, and charged, perhaps a little frightened.

"I can see a little better now," I said.

"We just stop here anyway and walk," the Bummer said. He pointed to the shell of a shack.

As we got closer and the fog grew thinner I could see that the shack was only two walls, each leaning into and supporting the other. The wood was old and gray, growing darker and browner near the ground where several boards were pried loose. A couple of bright green, laurel green, parrots sat on top of one wall, side by side, facing us. They didn't fly away as we drew closer and so I wondered if birds could fly in the fog, whether they were grounded.

The Bummer stood directly beneath the birds and pointed the muzzle of his black rifle at them. "Bang," he said. He turned and smiled at us. "Easy hunting. Anybody hungry?"

"We're good," Richard said.

I was surprised by how much relief I felt when he did not pull the trigger. I then realized just how tense my body had become. I tried to focus on my breathing, so that I could keep breathing. We walked on past the two walls and onto a trail that led down a hill through a stand of trees. It was damp in the thickly wooded area, but strangely warmer. Monkeys made sounds far off and parrots and other birds were calling more and more. I was several yards behind the Bummer, and Richard was crowding up behind me.

"Another goose chase?" Richard asked.

"Probably. I hope there's some food wherever we're going." I

looked at Richard and sighed. "You owe me big time." I looked at
the back of the Bummer's head, discovered I did not like the shape
of it. "Bummer, just where are we going? Fill us in on your method,
if you wouldn't mind."

The Bummer stopped, his shoulders sagged, and he sighed. He
turned around and looked at us, at me.

"I'm trying to find your friend's brother," he said, evenly.

"How?"

"If the missing boy is into drugs then I have to check out some
places."

"What kind of places?" Richard asked.

"Drug kind of places. Now what do you know? Not much, right?
Just let me do my job."

The trail ended at a narrow, yellowish dirt road, soaked from
rain. It was so rutted that it looked more like an old wagon trail, but
it was well scarred with the tracks of truck tires.

"This way," the Bummer said and led us left along the lane. I had
long ago lost any inkling of direction. With the fogginess I could not
even tell where the sun had come up. It started to drizzle, then it
rained harder. The water beat down on us. It rolled through my hair
and onto my face, which I had to keep wiping with my hand.

Ahead of us there were several huts and behind them a couple of
houses, a village. "Is this a village?" I asked.

The Bummer held his fist up by his head and crouched as he
moved toward the right side of the road. He was standing in an
ankle-deep puddle, but didn't seem to care or even notice. He held
his M16 differently now, his right hand on the trigger housing but his
finger away from the trigger. He walked slowly on and we followed.

I noticed a smell in the air, a burnt something, sulfur, a trace of
ammonia. The hair on my neck stood on end. Ahead of us, in the
middle of the muddy road, there appeared to be a garment, a sack, a
red sweater. Closer, it looked like a doll, but only momentarily. The
middle of it was sunk down into the mud. There were little feet, one
foot dressed in a sock and shoe. The face was turned away from us.

The Bummer stood erect and turned in a circle to see all around us, his finger tapping the trigger now.

"What the fuck?" I said. I started scanning the area. There was no sign of anyone else. "What the fuck is this?" I was staring at the Bummer, but he was paying no attention to me. He was peering down and up the lane and at the buildings.

"That's a kid," Richard said.

I nodded. I turned to see the body again and now I couldn't look away. Her blood was black mixed in with the mud, making a black and mustard soup, and she seemed to have been split in two like in a magician's act.

"That's a kid," Richard said again.

And again I nodded. "What the hell is going on here?" I asked the Bummer.

"Shut the fuck up," he said. "Keep your fucking eyes open."

"Where is everybody?" I asked.

"There was a lot of shooting here," the Bummer said. "Smell that powder. Ammonia in that stench—.223, smell it? Soldiers."

"Soldiers?" Richard said. "Christ."

The three of us jumped when we heard a clang, like a kicked pail, from behind a hut. My instinct was to get low and so I took a knee, but that put me closer to the dead child, a girl. Her dress was blue and her skin was the color of mine and she was framed by the stew her life had left in the mud. Her left hand was missing, an absence made more pronounced by the fact that her other hand had been washed clean by the rain and looked still alive. Richard stood behind the Bummer.

"*Salga!*" the Bummer shouted. "*Salga, ahora!*"

A small man and a very little boy walked out from behind the shack. They were shaking, soaked, unarmed. The Bummer lowered his rifle. He motioned for them to come closer, which they did.

"*Dónde está todo el mundo?*" the Bummer asked the man.

The man shook his head, tried to steal a peek at the body in the road.

"*Dónde está Carlos?*" The Bummer snapped his fingers in the man's face to get his attention. "Carlos."

"*No sé.*"

"Fuck," the Bummer said to no one in particular. He looked at the dead girl and back at the man. "*Su hija?*"

"*Sí.*"

"It's his kid," Richard said to me. And to himself.

Together, we all stood staring down at the girl. The man was crying, but making no sound. The boy was wide-eyed, silent, struck; he could have been four or a tiny seven, I didn't know. Then the man fell to pieces. Sinking to his knees, he covered his face with his muddy hands. He reached over and pulled the boy to him.

"Let's get the fuck out of here before whoever did this comes back," the Bummer said.

I looked at Richard. I had never seen him truly afraid before. "What are we supposed to do?" I asked.

Richard couldn't speak.

"We're supposed to get the fuck out of here," the Bummer said.

The little man got up and walked over to the outside wall of a nearby hut and grabbed a spade. He walked in a circle looking at the ground until he found a spot and started digging. The rain fell harder.

"Let's go," the Bummer said.

I didn't respond to him. I walked over and grabbed a square shovel from the same wall and joined the man in digging. Richard came over and took the spade from the father and he and I dug the grave together.

"You guys are fucking idiots," the Bummer said. He sat on a metal chair that had been left outside and kept watch. He kept saying *fuck* every few minutes. "Hurry the fuck up." He lit a cigarette and smoked in the rain. "Fuck."

"What are we doing here?" Richard asked me.

I tossed dirt out of the hole. "The only thing we can do." I didn't know if what I said was true. I didn't know if we were doing the right thing and frankly didn't care. I knew only that I had to do something, that I had to dig.

"I want to go home. Don't you want to go home?" Richard asked.

"I'm assuming that's rhetorical."

"Hurry the fuck up!" the Bummer shouted.

We kept digging, the wet earth offering no dust until we were a foot down. The digging became increasingly difficult as we got deeper and the color of the soil changed, became redder and rockier. There was a splinter between my thumb and forefinger, but I didn't care. I kept digging. I was focused on the digging because I didn't want to consider the child, the father.

I was crying when the man carried his daughter in pieces to the grave. He had taken off his yellow shirt and wrapped her head, covered her face. The wet fabric clung to her and I could still see her tiny features. I felt as if there was ice in my stomach. We didn't touch her, but let the man lay his daughter on the floor of the hole we'd made. The man took the spade from Richard and tossed in some dirt. He looked at me and added some more. I helped him cover her. My hands trembled the whole time, but the work, using the shovel, moving the dirt, steadied them.

When the grave was about half full, and a grave is never half empty, I noticed that the rain had stopped. I leaned on the shovel to rest, looked at the sliver deep in my flesh. The boy came to me, offered me something, confused me, then I realized that he was giving me his sister's left hand. It had not made it into the grave, but must have been lost in the mud and blood puddle. His shirt was cobalt blue. The severed hand was fairly blue black. There was no red to be seen, as if blood was never red. The father did not see me take the hand. In my own hand the piece of a person felt like a feather, a wet nothing. Before the man turned to see it, I dropped it into the grave and covered it. Richard didn't see what had happened. The Bummer was quietly sitting guard, smoking another cigarette. I shared this with the boy and the boy alone. I was never told his name, but in my mind, in my story, in my world, his name was Luis.

Paris

The air was much cooler than it had been, but the heat lamp made our sitting outside more than comfortable. Victoire ordered a coffee, crossed her legs, and leaned against me in a familiar way that I did not expect.

"So, you have remained for me," she said.

I said nothing. I had remained because of my gallerist's request, but I could not tell her that she was wrong. I accepted her pleasant weight against me and watched the traffic.

Once her coffee had arrived and she had blown on it and taken a sip, Victoire sighed and said, "Are we going to sit here all day?"

"We just got here."

"You're afraid of me."

"I am." My honesty made me feel better.

"Then let's not go to your hotel. Let's not go to my place. Where should we go?" All of this in a calm, quiet voice that was musical.

"Let's go to the Musée d'Art Moderne," I suggested.

"You said that very well," she said.

"Thank you. I've been practicing." I looked at the clouds. "There's a taxi stand over there or we could walk over to the river."

"Or we could get on this bus," she said, nodding toward a bus just half a block away.

"This bus here?"

"*Oui.*"

I put money on the table and we boarded the bus. Like a couple of kids, we went straight to the back. The bus moved before we were settled and we lost our balance. Victoire held on to my hand and I fell laughing into the seat beside her. We were still laughing when I thought I heard someone call my name.

"Kevin? Kevin Pace?"

The moderately high yet raspy voice attached to my name was female, familiar but not readily identifiable, though in less time than it takes to make a mistake, the face behind the voice was all too clear. The grating voice belonged to Melissa Lowry, not truly a neighbor, but close enough to annoy like a neighbor. I had gone months without seeing her and yet here she was in Paris. She was a professor of sociology at Brown, no more than an acquaintance, but familiar enough that I dropped Victoire's soft hand. I felt the young woman sink, if not into the seat, certainly into herself, and so I too sank.

"Kevin Pace, what are you doing here?" Melissa Lowry asked.

"Taking the bus," I said.

Melissa Lowry looked at Victoire. "And who is your friend?"

"Victoire, this is Melissa Lowry, a neighbor from back home. Melissa, this is Victoire." I realized that I didn't know Victoire's last name and when I looked at her, as if to find it, Victoire looked all of seventeen years old. I turned back to Melissa, perhaps a little quickly, and said, "Victoire is a watercolorist."

"I'm sure she is," Melissa Lowry said.

"We're on our way to the Musée d'Art Moderne," I said, but my accent suffered from the stress so that even I could hear it. I said it as if going there suggested innocence, like going to temple or church.

"Well, I hope you enjoy it," Melissa Lowry said and turned back around in her seat.

Victoire would not look at my eyes and if she had I would have had a difficult time holding them. I didn't know whether I had hurt her or embarrassed her or disappointed her. I had certainly disappointed myself. Worse, now I was afraid. Finally, however, I collected myself. I imagined linen newly stretched over bars and my fear dissipated. I nudged Victoire gently and when she glanced at me, I nodded toward the back of Melissa Lowry's head and whispered. "Boudin."

This made Victoire laugh. I laughed, too, and felt immediately better, better still when I could see that our laughter confused Melissa Lowry, perhaps even caused her a modicum of discomposure.

We rose to exit at the Musée des Égouts de Paris. I even said a happy good-bye to Melissa Lowry as I passed. I never saw her face. In fact, I don't think I ever saw Melissa Lowry's face again.

We crossed the Seine on the Pont de l'Alma. We stopped in the middle and looked down at the water and over at the gaudy vessels of the Bateaux-Mouches.

"We should take a boat ride," I said.

"That is for tourists," she said.

"I am a tourist."

"You are not a tourist. You are with a young, beautiful French girl." She bounced away. I should have felt the residual sting of that embarrassment on the bus, but I did not. I felt light.

In the museum, we stood quietly then sat quietly for a very long time in front of Picasso's *Le pigeon aux petits pois*. I of course loved the yellows and the small places of mustard and it thrilled me when Victoire calmly found the peas and then the dove.

Some ten years later the painting would be stolen by a man who simply shattered a window and entered the museum. I wondered when I learned of the theft how I might have seen the painting that day with Victoire and, more, I wondered how I might have viewed my hours with that young woman. The interesting thing about the work was that I did not love it. The interesting thing about the woman was that I did.

"What shall we look at now?" she asked, still staring at the Picasso.

We walked into a large room with works by Metzinger and Lhote and I was nonplussed, the way artists can be unmoved by art, a feeling that always made me a little sad, a little ashamed.

But then Victoire began to step from marble tile to marble tile, a dance between the cracks. "I think this floor is beautiful," she said. "*Et regarde le banc simple blanc.*"

I looked at the bench. It was three faces of a rectangular box. It was simple. It was the most beautiful thing in the room.

She ran and sat on it, placed her palms flat against it. "Who do you think made it?" she asked.

"I wish I knew," I said and I meant it.

House

I was chopping carrots for the salad when Linda came in with sacks of groceries. She hoisted them onto the counter.

"Any more in the car?" I asked.

"Four."

"I'll get them." I dried my hands on a towel and made eye contact with April as she entered the kitchen. I went out to the car and grabbed two bags and brought them inside. April had taken over chopping the carrots. Linda was putting away the groceries and they were not speaking. Will rode up on his bicycle as I closed the back of the station wagon.

"Hey, kiddo."

"Let me take one of those."

"Thanks. How was school?"

"What do you think I'm going to say?"

"Fine," I said.

"Fine," he repeated. "This is where you say, 'Is it always simply fine?'"

"As a matter of fact." I held the door open for him. "Doesn't anything interesting ever happen at that school?"

"Nope."

"The gym teacher has never been caught spying on girls through a hole in the shower wall?"

"Never caught," he laughed.

April was done with the salad and sitting at the counter with a glass of water. "Hey, twerp," she said to her brother.

"Original," Will said.

April put her glass down a little heavily, leaned forward slightly, her arm on the counter.

"You okay, honey?" Linda asked.

"I'm fine," April said. She sat up and breathed deeply, deliberately. "I'll be right back."

"She doesn't look good," Linda said when April was out of the room.

"Understatement," Will said.

"Is she all right?" Linda asked. "She seems really nervous lately."

"She's always nervous," Will said. "Hormones."

I gave Will a brief glance, wondering if he knew what I knew, but it was clear he didn't. "That's enough, Will."

"I'm just saying, it must be tough becoming a woman and all." Will took glasses from the cabinet and took them to the table.

"Maybe I should go check on her," Linda said.

"I'll go," I said. This came as a surprise to Linda and she gave me something just shy of a sidelong glance.

By the time I made my way down the hall, April was out of the bathroom and in her room sitting on her bed. I sat beside her. "Pretty rough?" I asked.

"The last two days."

"Let me ask you, did you take a test or go to the doctor? I mean, are you sure you're pregnant?" I put my arm around her.

"I'm sure."

"You need to see a doctor."

"I'm not keeping it. I'm sixteen years old."

I paused to listen for footsteps in the hall. I saw the neighbor's cat walk across the roof outside April's window. "I really hate that cat," I said.

"Me too," April said.

"Think hard about this, sweetheart." I gave her shoulder a squeeze.

"You haven't told her, have you?"

"I haven't, but I really need to, April."

"Please, don't."

"April."

"Please, Dad."

"She's going to have to know eventually."

"Why?"

"Because she has to, that's why. She's your mother."

April held my hand. And though it was only seconds before Will shouted out for us to come to the table, that moment felt luxurious, orchestrated. Her hand was still a child's hand, still my child's hand. I slid my thumb across her knuckles.

"Are you guys coming?" Will called.

"On our way," I said.

We arrived at the table to find Will and Linda already serving themselves.

"Everything okay?" Linda asked.

"Everything's fine," April said.

Linda looked at me. It was an accusing look that I didn't understand and yet I did. Perhaps she suspected somehow that April was pregnant, a mother's intuition. Perhaps she was simply jealous that I was somehow at that moment closer to our daughter than she was. Certainly she was aware that there was a secret, something, in the air.

"Feeling better?" Linda asked.

"Fine, I'm fine. Allergies, I think. I was feeling a bit dizzy."

"I was congested today too," I said.

Linda smiled and nodded, but it was not a pleasant smile. "There is a change in the weather," she said.

1979

The walk away from the grave was silent and blank. It seemed that all color had left the world. Richard and I couldn't speak; we wouldn't speak. But the Bummer just wouldn't shut up, even though he was apparently on alert. He kept us off the road in the trees.

"That was some shit, wasn't it?" His voice was just above a whisper. "Soldiers, man, these fucking soldiers. They'll shoot anybody. They like to shoot. That ammonia we smelled, .223 rounds, M16s like my baby right here, the only powder that stinks like that. I shouldn't say stink. It's not a bad smell. I feel sorry for that man back there. Little girl like that. I got a little sister back home. She's a nurse now, lives in Virginia. Probably not a very good nurse. She was never very smart. Watch out for snakes out here. There are some really nasty ones. The coral snakes don't get upset easily and they're not up this high anyway. But those vipers. Some of them jump. Ever seen a snake jump?"

"Shut the fuck up," I said.

"Excuse me?" he said.

"I said shut the fuck up."

"Do you know who could be in this bush? I'm the one who's going to keep you breathing."

"Get us killed," Richard said.

"And who the hell is Carlos?" I asked.

"Do you still want my help?" he asked, in a steady, soft voice, seemingly, ironically, sincere. "Do you still want your brother?" He tilted his head as he looked at Richard's face.

Richard's shoulders sagged. "Yes."

"Good, now if you girls will just follow me." We fell in behind him, moving quickly and keeping low. "Keep your eyes open."

"Bummer, who is Carlos?" I asked.

"He's my contact."

"Contact? What the fuck is a contact?"

We came to the trail that had led us to the road where the Bummer broke into a trot. We ran all the way back to the car. I started to fall in behind the wheel, but the Bummer stopped me.

"I want him to drive," he said.

"Why?" Richard asked.

"I like the way you drive. And I don't like him." He cut me a hard look. Strange, even in the moment, I found the look almost comical and I must have smiled slightly because he said, "What's so funny?"

I looked at his rifle. "Nothing."

Back in the cantina. For the first time I realized the place was windowless. The same bartender served us the same beer.

The Bummer sat across from us. He drummed on the table with his thumbs. "I hate that my cooler is empty. This donkey piss they serve in here will kill you." He laughed and took a pull on his bottle. He scratched at the label with a nail. "Regia," he read. "What's that Spanish for?"

"*Royal*, maybe," Richard said, half interested.

"No, dumbshit, it means donkey piss. I just told you that." The Bummer stopped, listened. "Shit."

"What is it?" Richard asked.

"Company."

The door was pulled open and loud voices came in before the soldiers. The uniformed men were sloppy and boisterous, stomping mud off their boots and laughing. The Bummer watched them conspicuously.

"Be cool," he said. "This ain't nothing."

"Do you think—" I started a question.

"Shut up." The Bummer shoved his rifle under the table and laid it gently on the floor.

The bartender didn't seem surprised to see the soldiers, but he wasn't pleased by their presence. He had much the same manner as

he had had with the Bummer. He served them at the bar, but didn't
laugh with them. Two of the soldiers sat in the other booth. A soldier looked over from the bar and made eye contact with me and I
of course looked away. He nudged the man next to him, said something, and then walked across the room.

The Bummer picked him up halfway and tossed up a big wave.
"Hola," he said. *"Cómo estás?"*

"Americans," the man said.

"Yep," the Bummer said.

"And you, you are the one they call Bummer."

The Bummer winked at us. "I'm famous." To the soldier, "That's
me."

"And who are these men?"

"Friends."

"Why are you out here?"

"We're tourists."

The soldier's eyes stayed on us. Something in his physical attitude must have spoken to the others because they stopped talking
and looked our way. The soldier at our table looked back at the
Bummer, paused a beat, and then laughed. *"Este es el Bummer,"* he
said loudly. He smiled at us and returned to the bar. I was both
drawn to and repulsed by the olive drab color of their presence and
of a sudden I was aware that the only bright color in the place was
the remaining neon letters of the beer sign. I couldn't help but enter
into an analysis of the color, how to make it, it helped me relax.
Olive drab. Cadmium orange and halo blue or perhaps ocher with
gray, maybe Payne's gray. Thunder rumbled far off.

"What are you doing?" Richard asked.

"What?"

"You keep staring at those soldiers and they're going to come
back over here," he said.

"Your girlfriend is nervous," the Bummer said to me.

The door opened again and I could hear the rain. A white guy came stomping through the doorway, shaking off a poncho. He was dressed in cowboy boots, jeans, and a loud pink polo shirt. He looked around confidently and nodded to the soldiers, who seemed to not care about him at all; at least they were not surprised to see him. He looked over and saw the Bummer, smiled broadly.

"*Amigo*," he said with an accent worse than mine. "Bummer, imagine finding you here." He spoke English with what I thought was a German accent. He fell easily onto the bench next to the Bummer. He carried a fat ring-binder notebook that he put on the table. After an awkward silence the man said, "Aren't you going to introduce me to your comrades?"

"Comrades, this is Carlos. Ricky and Kurt."

"I take it Carlos is not your real name," Richard said.

"I hope that Ricky is not yours," he said. "Real names are no good when there's a war going on."

"This is Carlos, the one we've been looking for?"

The Bummer nodded.

"So, do your thing," Richard said. "Ask him about my brother."

"Brother?" Carlos said.

"You want a beer?" the Bummer asked.

"I'm all right," Carlos said. "Brother?"

"Ricky here is looking for his brother. He came down here to score drugs and turned up missing, as they say."

"So he wants to look at the book?"

"The book?" Richard said.

"Two hundred," Carlos said.

"What?" Richard looked at me and then back at the man.

"American dollars. And that's a special for you because you're a friend of the Bummer."

"He's not my friend," Richard said. "And I don't have any money with me and what the fuck are you talking about?"

"No money, no book." Carlos draped his arm over his notebook.

"What the fuck are you talking about?" I asked. "What's a notebook have to do with anything?"

"Doesn't matter," Carlos said. "No money. Doesn't mean we can't have a party."

He called back to the bartender, *"Señor, el whiskey, por favor!"*

Even after a few shots of what passed for whiskey it would have been a cliché to claim that the scene was surreal; it would also have been a lie. The loud soldiers, all of that khaki, the muddy boot prints on the floor, the cold fire, the grunting, laughing, and shouting. It was real enough, not at all dreamlike, though plenty strange. I kept expecting the colors of the place to be different from home, but none were. The people were the same color as the people at home. The furniture was the same color. Even the spider monkeys in the trees were the color of dogs, collies and pit bulls from Baltimore Avenue. And yet we stood out like we were painted cobalt blue. I kept seeing the tiny dead girl, her lost brother, her distraught father. I knew that this country was ready to explode but I had no idea what that meant exactly, how it would look. Little things and big things, bad things happen in singular moments, in singularly real places, not points on a map, not in regions.

"So, what are you? German?" I asked Carlos.

"Dutch."

"How did you come to be here?"

"I take pictures," he said. "I'm a photojournalist."

"For a newspaper?" Richard asked.

"Freelance," he said.

I smiled, didn't quite laugh, but Carlos saw my reaction.

"I'm a photojournalist," he repeated.

I thought about the boy, Luis, and felt anger. I found the Bummer's eyes and surprised him by not looking away.

"What?" he said.

"Tell me the name of that village?" I asked.

"What?"

"Today. Where were we? What's the name of that village?"

"Who the fuck cares," the Bummer said, waving me off. "Toledo.

How about that? Toledo sounds Spanish, right?" He looked at Richard. "Is Toledo a Spanish word?"

"What is it called?" I asked, my voice slightly louder. I could feel my voice in my head, my chest.

"Keep your voice down," the Bummer said to me.

For the first time I felt I had some power over him, but even drunk I realized that to exploit it would be to my detriment.

"Better yet," he said, "just shut the fuck up."

I didn't shut the fuck up. "Tell me," I said, louder than I intended.

The Bummer put his pistol on the table and rested his hand on it, the barrel pointed not at me but at Richard. He smiled. "I learned a long time ago that you don't threaten the threat, you threaten the family."

I said nothing, but sank back into the bench. I looked at Richard's face, apologized with my eyes. "I want to know the name of the village," I said, softly. "Please."

"I said it doesn't fucking matter. Now, sit back and shut the fuck up."

Carlos watched all of this calmly. "What happened today?" he asked. He put a cigarette into his mouth and offered one to the Bummer, not to either of us.

"Nothing," I said.

"Doesn't sound like nothing," Carlos said.

I looked at Richard. He was drunker than I was, looked ready to puke. "We dug a grave," I said.

"Were you in Las Salinas?" Carlos asked. "Tell me you weren't there."

"Not all the way," the Bummer said.

"Is that the name?" I asked. "Las Salinas."

"Time to stop talking," the Bummer said, glancing about the room. He leaned forward. "Maybe these soldiers were in that village today. Maybe they think that nobody knows what happened. Maybe they think that there are no witnesses."

That scared me close to death. I stared at my half-empty glass, didn't consider even a furtive glance around the room.

Richard leaned toward me and said, "This shit taste like earwax." He threw it back, then out of a tight throat, "Definitely, earwax."

He and I laughed. Carlos swallowed his drink. I did the same.

The Bummer watched us laughing. He held his glass up as if admiring the color of the whiskey. He slowly put the glass to his lips. "I like earwax," he said and drank the contents of his glass very slowly.

We laughed again, harder this time, but the Bummer did not. He just closed his eyes and settled into the corner as if for a nap.

Paris

At that moment of seeing Victoire childlike on that bench I could have caught myself, freed myself with even the mildest allusion to *Lolita*, but the fact of the matter was that it was not her youth that attracted me. In fact, I am not even certain that what charmed me was all that genuine, that being her guiltlessness, her irreproachability, either of which were constructions of mine or hers. It really wasn't that I wanted her, but that I wanted what she had, a kind of freedom, a purity of spirit. It was a sort of integrity, something that I strived for but had lost through so many years, maybe never had. I wanted what she had the way I wanted to draw the way my daughter drew when she was four, when that tangle of lines was an elephant, an elephant that I could not see, but an elephant. I recalled how brokenhearted I was when one day she crumpled up her picture and complained that it didn't look like an elephant at all. Victoire allowed me to see that simple bench as it was, as more than what it was, and I was happy for it. I loved her for it. I sat on it beside her and felt the smoothness of it under my palms, attended to the coolness of it.

"Where shall we go now?" she asked.

"The aquarium is not far away," I said.

"You're afraid of *us*."

That she said *us* instead of *me* was not unnoticed and I was impressed because she was correct. "That's probably true," I said.

"I have nice tea at my flat."

"Do you?"

"It is Iranian tea," she said.

I looked across the room at a canvas and didn't recognize the hand that had made it, but what was interesting was that I didn't care and, more, I found the painting boring, flat, uninspired, and then I found the whole museum that way.

"You know," I said. "I've come to dislike museums."

"Why is that?" she asked.

"It's where art comes to die. Look at this place. It's a crypt."

"That's sad."

"Look at those people over there, nice people, smart people, viewing the dead in open caskets."

I could feel Victoire looking at me. "That's the most you have ever said all at once."

"I don't know what's gotten into me."

"My place?" she asked.

"Okay." I agreed because that was what I wanted.

At this point there was no need or reason to resort to philosophical reflection. Waiting and suspense were predictable, perhaps necessary characteristics of the situation, *situation* being both an unfortunate and an extremely accurate term. Delay and anxious uncertainty, sine qua non. All the way to Victoire's apartment, however, I did not think about how I might kiss her that second time. I instead wondered how we would talk, though that wonder did not manifest as some interior rehearsal. I simply wondered and that pleased me.

As we entered her building I sensed if not doubt then at least some apprehension in Victoire. This seemed reasonable enough to me, but it didn't come across as a function of her youth, but rather as a concern for me. I felt it and appreciated it, was actually impressed by it. By the time we were up the two flights and inside her apartment she had put her hand on my arm.

"Ça va?"

"I'm fine. You?"

"I am very fine. I don't have a wife."

"This, what we have here, is ours." It sounded like such a line, but I had talked myself into believing that very thing. Just inside her door, I said, "Still, you understand this is what it is."

"You think too much," she said.

"And I talk too much."

She touched my face. I touched hers.

What was wonderful was that the sex was tender, that we kissed, that we were slow, that we were a little clumsy, a lot clumsy when it came to the condom, my clumsiness and the object itself making me self-aware, embarrassed, a bit ashamed. But that faded when she kissed me. I imagined in the middle of it all that I would be less ungainly, a bit more graceful in bed the next time. I loved being inside her and somehow felt I was not experiencing it fully, that the moment was getting away from me, that it was all rushed, but it was not, time was what time is, its own pace. She moved and she didn't move, every sound was sweet to me. I didn't know where her hands were most of the time, but I did know they pleased me. She might have had an orgasm, but I didn't care.

"If you were to paint our sex, would it be a big canvas?" she asked. She stared at the ceiling.

"*Demandes-tu en français,*" I said.

"*Si tu étais à peindre notre sexe, dirais-tu peindre une grande toile?*"

I rolled onto my back, laughed softly.

"That was funny?" she said.

"That was beautiful," I told her. "Yes, it would be a large canvas. However, it would be part of a canvas."

"Will you paint it?"

"*Oui.*"

"*Ton français est parfait.*"

I picked up my watch from the nightstand and checked the time.

"Do you have to leave?"

"I don't know," I said. "I *will* have to go back to my hotel."

"I know."

I sat up and started to get dressed even though I didn't have to rush out. It just seemed like what I ought to do, realizing that the act of leaving was going to be awkward whenever it happened. At least I thought it would be awkward. Victoire subverted that expectation.

"I will miss you," she said. She cuddled up to my back. "Will I see you tomorrow?"

"Would you like to see me tomorrow?"

"That is a very silly question. Before you go, I would like you to tell me a secret."

"What kind of secret?"

"A real secret. We will tell each other secrets."

"You first."

"Okay." She kissed the back of my neck and pulled herself around to sit next to me. "My boyfriend does not know that you are here."

I was surprised by her secret and just a little amused at the fear that ran through me right then. "I guess I'm relieved to hear that. Where does he live? Does he like to just stop by?"

"He's not much of a boyfriend. He is, after all, just a boy. He is going to leave me. I know this."

"Why would he leave you?" My question was an honest one.

"I don't know. He worries too much." She held my hand up to her face and looked at it.

"Why do you think he's going to leave you?"

"I just know it."

"People tend to worry when they care."

"Perhaps. Now, your secret."

"You. You are my secret," I said.

She studied me for a few seconds. "Tomorrow night, after you fuck me, we will have tea and you will tell me a better secret."

House

We lived at either the edge of the country or the edge of town, either way being equally unimpressive as the so-called country consisted of large houses with gigantic yards and a smattering of horses and the so-called town was little more than a hamlet, being made up mostly of large houses with smaller yards. Straddling the two, our house was enough town to have a smaller yard and enough country to have a large enough yard for the two outbuildings that served as my studios. It was all very arty and New Englandy.

This to introduce what was called the Feedstore or more precisely Frazar's Feedstore. It was a half mile from my house. On weekends upscale ruralites and weekend equestrian-garment wearers would park their mostly German cars on the gravel yard and rub well-heeled elbows while drinking coffee from paper cups on the wide porch. They would yawn, stretch, and breathe in the air and complain about city life, Boston or Providence, the latter though hardly a city had its share of city problems, while oblivious to the fact that the family who owned and worked the store fairly hated them. Perhaps hate is too strong a word, the Frazars being aware of their bread and which side the butter was on and all that, but still they did not like the crowd of patrons terribly much, if at all. The Frazars delivered timothy grass, alfalfa, and oat hay to the pristine and spotless barns and sold them overpriced bags of food for their Labradors and Weimaraners, and managed cordiality and courtesy, but I knew. They might have hated me, and perhaps they did and I just couldn't tell, oblivious like the folks on the porch, but I wanted to believe that my relationship with them was somehow different. To the Frazars I was the crazy artist who lived down the lane. They liked that I walked to their place in paint-splattered work boots and overalls and drank their coffee and actually complained about it on occasion. My lunch every day was two of their pre-foil-wrapped hot dogs that they heated in some kind of oven; that alone should have given me the credibility I imagined. That I ate shit for lunch, walked, and was dirty from work, even if it was paint, should have made me more acceptable. I enjoyed at least the perception that they liked me.

One weekday I made the trek there for my lunch. While I ate my second dog I perused a wall of horse bits. The bits themselves were interesting, beautiful, even the ones that looked so blatantly painful, like the one made from a segment of bicycle chain, it having been there since long before I moved into my house, but the wall of them was magnificent. I had no desire to paint likenesses of horse bits, but there was something about all of them there together, so alike and so different, so beautiful and cruel, circles and eggbutts and D-rings, so the yellowed labels told me. A few steps farther and I was facing a tangle of ocher-colored hoses and a very large white plastic barrel. The tag on it claimed it was a stable fly suppression system.

The teenage Frazar was marking inventory on a clipboard just a couple of feet away. His name was Jason and I knew this because of his embroidered shirt, though I had seen him many times.

"What is this?" I asked.

"That, Mr. Pace, is a stable fly suppression system," he said cheerfully as if I couldn't read.

I bit off some hot dog. "Well, Jason, I can see that." I pointed at the tag. "What does it do?"

"It suppresses flies," he said.

"*Suppress* being euphemistic for *kill*. I don't mind the idea of killing flies at all and we're not in the CIA."

"You put fly spray in this drum here and you see it's on this timer and every however-long-you-want it shoots the fly spray around the barn and . . ."

"Suppresses the flies."

"Exactly."

"Suppresses them to death," I said.

"That's the idea."

"How much does a suppressing thing like this cost?" I finished my dog and touched the tangle of hoses.

"I think it's around two fifty." He looked at me. "You don't have horses, do you?"

I shook my head.

"You got a lot of flies around your place?"

"Not especially. No more than anyone else, I guess." I paused to study young Jason's face. "You're a friend of my daughter."

"Yes, sir." He looked back down at his clipboard. "April and I went out a couple of times."

I felt like a bad father for not knowing that, but I recalled at that moment having heard the name Jason used in our kitchen. It then struck me that Jason Frazar might be the boy who had gotten my little girl pregnant. That of course would have occurred to me if any boy had told me he knew my daughter. It seemed like too much of a coincidence that this kid right now might be the one, but I couldn't shake the notion. I stared at him.

"That thing has been sitting around collecting dust for a while," he said. "I bet my dad would give you a good deal on it."

I was still staring at him.

"On the fly outfit," he said.

"Yeah, I'll think about it."

I watched the boy walk away, but I was not thinking about him and his possible guilt so much as I was lamenting my situation. I needed to tell Linda, but every minute that passed without my telling her made it that much more difficult. Yes, April would hate me and for some reason, in spite of the fact that I believed she already hated me on some level, I couldn't stomach the idea that I would have broken a promise to her. I wondered if our secret, my knowing while her mother did not, my helping with the doctor and all, would actually remain a secret or whether it might become an item for blackmail down the road or perhaps a weapon of mass destruction to pull out against her mother one day.

I regarded the stable fly suppression system and imagined the drum full of sodium hydroxide and the yellowish tubing stretched along the top of my private painting. The opening of the door could flip the switch and the system could then apply the caustic soda over the canvas and thereby ruin and perhaps erase my painting before anyone could see it. I became excited by the idea, perhaps disproportionately excited, no doubt a deflection of the business that was so pressing and troubling.

"Jason," I called to the boy who was now making the silage forks neat in their bin. "Jason, where is your father?"

"You really want that thing?"

"I think so."

"He's up in the office. I'll go get him."

The elder Frazar was a big man. I have big hands, but his mitt engulfed mine when we shook. I didn't know him to be a wheeler-dealer, but then I hadn't bought anything but coffee, hot dogs, and the occasional garden tool from him.

"So, you got yourself a fly problem," he said. "This here is a very nice little system."

"Do you think I might have a discount?" I asked right away.

"It's listed at two seventy."

That was more than Jason had said, but he was not being precise, I understood that. "Would you take two hundred?"

Frazar smiled. "I don't think so. Tell you what, let's say two fifty and call it good. How's that sound?"

"Sounds like retail," I said.

"Two forty," he said.

I looked at Jason, who had come to stand behind his father, and the thought flashed again that he might be the father of my grandson and that would make old man Frazar related to me in whatever way those things worked. I wondered if he knew about April's condition. I abandoned our negotiation and said to Jason, "When is the last time you saw April?"

He was taken completely off guard, as well he should have been, my question coming out of left field like that. "I saw her about a week ago."

I nodded. They didn't attend the same school.

Father Frazar cleared his throat.

I returned my attention to the older man. "Two forty is fine. Do you think you could deliver it?"

"Today?"

"That would be great."

"I can be there around four. You want me to fill the drum with insecticide?"

"No, but I'd like ten gallons of sodium hydroxide."

"Beg pardon?"

"Ten gallons of sodium hydroxide."

"We'll have it there." The man nodded to his son to start packing up the merchandise. "All we have is one-gallon jugs of the sodium hydroxide. I don't know if we have ten of them."

"Whatever you have. I'll pay you when you come over. I don't have my wallet on me."

"No worries."

"Tell April I said hello," Jason said.

"I will," I said.

1979

Richard and I still sat right next to each other in the car, but couldn't talk about what had happened that day. Even if the Bummer and Carlos had left us there alone we were too drunk on earwax whiskey to discuss anything. I'm not certain what any discussion would have done to make any of what he had witnessed or done make more sense, but at least we could have verified that we had been through the same things. In the small hours I came to twice, once to observe that the Bummer was mouth-open-sound-asleep and still seated across from me and that a wide-eyed Carlos was staring at me. "So, what's in the notebook?" I asked. If he did answer, I didn't hear him. I glanced over to see Richard head down on the table. I don't know if he answered me. The second time I awoke to see three women talking to the drunken soldiers and I assumed that they were prostitutes, felt briefly bad for the assumption, and then thought, of course they were prostitutes. I don't think that I was ever really asleep, not that it mattered, as I was completely unaware of my surrounds, and yet somehow I managed to awake in the backseat of the Cadillac. It was barely light out and there was no fog this morning, so not only was the front of the cantina plainly visible, but so were the flatbed truck and two Jeeps that had no doubt brought the soldiers. One soldier leaned against the truck and smoked, perhaps on guard duty. He glanced over at me with indifference laced with disdain, looked at his cigarette and then back toward the road.

The Bummer and Carlos walked out of the cantina, looking fresher than they should have. Richard followed, looking like I felt. I got out of the car.

"Give me the keys," the Bummer said to me.

"I've got the keys," Richard told him. "And why should I give them to you? So you can leave us here."

"You want your fucking brother or not?" The Bummer tilted his head left, then right. "I'm out here for fucking you. I could be back at my place scoring some Salvadoran pussy. Now, give me the goddamn keys."

Richard handed over the keys.

"Get in the goddamn backseat," he said.

Richard and I did just that. Carlos rode shotgun. Richard and I came around slowly, but not before Richard vomited out the window. I nearly did the same and wished in fact that I had. By now I had lost all sense of direction and had no idea where we were.

"Hey, Carlos," I called from the backseat.

He looked back.

"What's in the notebook?"

"What is it with you?" the Bummer asked. "It's not your brother who's lost. Why'd you come here?"

"What's in the notebook?" I asked again.

Carlos looked at the Bummer and they cracked up laughing.

Four hours later and I thought I recognized the countryside, but I didn't trust my eyes. I nudged Richard awake.

"Does this look familiar?" I asked.

He nodded. "We're near the city."

He was right. Soon I realized that we were approaching the slums where the Bummer lived. "We are back," I said.

"So, this is it," Richard said. "What about my brother?"

"I'm working on it."

"Working on it?"

"Yeah, you boys take your car back to where you're staying and get some rest," the Bummer said. "What hotel are you in?"

Richard looked at me and shrugged. "The Hotel Terraza."

The Bummer stopped the car in front of his trailer. "The Hotel Terraza. I'll find you when I know something."

"So what was the point of us going all the way out there with you?" I nodded toward the mountains.

"Go get some rest," he said.

Richard and I hardly spoke on the way into town. As he parked the Cadillac in the same spot, he apologized again.

"Don't," I said. "This isn't your fault. It's not even my fucking fault for agreeing to come. We're here and that's that."

"We buried somebody," Richard said to the steering wheel.

"Yeah."

"I'm really undone right now," he said.

I looked through the windshield at the quiet afternoon streets. "This place is about to blow up and we're in the middle of it."

"What are you saying?"

"Don't look at me. He's your brother. If you want to find him, I'm with you. It's your call."

"I think we should just go to the airport."

"What about your mother?" I asked.

He shrugged.

"Sleep on it. Decide in the morning." I sounded like a good friend was supposed to sound and perhaps I was being one, but my decision to leave it up to him was a complicated one. Of course I had been deeply affected by what had happened the previous day, but I had shared something with Luis, a boy I didn't know, whose name I had made up, that I could not articulate. The royal blue of his shirt was still with me. The sound he had made was no sound, no sound at all. I looked at myself. I was sweaty, bloody, muddy and wore the sickly sweet smell of an alcoholic uncle. I wanted to go to sleep in the shower.

When Richard came out of the shower he stood naked in the middle of the room and said, "Are we going to talk about this?"

"Sure, you're moderately well hung. How's that?"

"Not that." He pulled on his pants. "About what happened."

"What's there to say? We helped a man bury his murdered daughter. We rode around the bush with a fucking lunatic. We got drunk on who-knows-what and came back to this lovely hotel. Do you have anything to add?" I realized just then how sore my shoulders were from the digging.

"No."

"I need to take a shower. And I'm going to be in there for a very, very long time."

"What do you think we should do?"

I leaned against the doorjamb. "I say let's cut our losses and get the fuck out of here. But as to whether I'll stay and help find Tad, you know the answer to that. He's your brother and you're my friend."

"Okay."

"Go get us some food while I'm in there."

"I'll find us something."

While I was standing in the shower, while the hot water ran out, while I adjusted to the cold water, I imagined that I might cry, but I didn't. I washed my hair.

Paris

The gallery in Paris that represented my work was on the short rue Visconti between rue Bonaparte and rue de Seine. It was unassuming from the outside, the front window being smallish and not revealing much, but once you were inside the space opened remarkably, tall white walls rising to a gabled glass roof. The gallerist Etienne Bauer was a beautiful man, handsome in a way that I might have envied. Though he was larger than I was, I felt lumbering next to him. And poorly dressed as well. His jackets and scarves that matched his socks seemed so natural that I looked as if I had intentionally dressed down. He and I were standing in front of a large canvas of mine, an unusual one for me, it having many reds. To tell the truth I never thought I had control of the work, but he liked it enough to place it so as to be seen through the window.

He pointed out a region of the painting that had been my least favorite and said, "There is an urgent movement of grief here somehow posed as a rhetorical question." His hand kept moving, floating. "And here, we have similarly constructed subordinate clauses." He looked at my face, then back at the painting. "Of which this one is much broader in scope."

I wanted to think that he was actually seeing something and that he was merely articulating it poorly in English, but I knew that it was all bullshit. But then maybe it wasn't.

"*Dans un mois, dans un an, comment souffrirons-nous, Seigneur, que tant de Mers me séparent de vous,*" he said.

"*Bérénice,*" I said, recognizing the Racine only because he had written the line to me in a letter about this very painting.

"*Très bon.* What shall we call it?" he asked.

"What about *Bérénice*?" I said.

"*Génial.* That is perfect."

So it was done. A painting I didn't care for had a title and I had stroked the ego of my gallerist by letting him believe he had planted the idea in my head. And of course he had. I turned to look out the window and was thrown off as I saw Victoire bounce into view. She glanced my way, offered a sudden smile with her eyes, and walked on with a suggestion of stopping.

"She is beautiful," Etienne said. "Do you know her?"

I lied.

"Paris is full of them," he said and sighed. "Perhaps too many."

I returned my gaze to the painting.

"Let's have some tea," he said.

I looked again through the window and then followed him to the back. I sat at the table while he put on water.

"It is almost Christmas," Etienne said. "I do not like Christmas."

"Why is that? Paris is so beautiful during the season."

"Do you think so? I find it all garish. Is that the correct word? In French I would say *criard, voyant.*"

"*Garish* is correct," I said. "Gaudy."

"*Gaudy,* that's the word I was looking for. All the lights and tinsel. It is not for me. I like a separation of things, high and low. Jesus screwed it all up. *Il a détruit la séparation entre le sublime et le quotidien.*"

"Is that an allusion to something I should know?" I asked.

"No, I just made it up. I quite like it."

I was too nervous to sit still. I was bothered by having seen Victoire through the window and wanted very much to chase after her.

"*Ça va?*"

"I really need to go, Etienne."

"But you haven't had your tea."

"I'll take a rain check."

"What does it mean, *rain check*?"

"We'll have tea at a later date. Tomorrow. I have to go now." I grabbed my coat and hurried out.

Outside I walked east toward rue de Seine and there I turned south. I walked with a deliberate stride toward the Boulevard Saint-Germain, becoming sad and angry, wondering how she could have been so dismissive of my need for discretion. I did not actually think that I would see her, but I did. She was sitting at an outdoor table at a café sipping an espresso. I stood next to her.

"Kevin," she said, happy to see me.

"What was that?" I asked.

"*Pardon?*"

"What was that all about? Are you following me now?" I asked.

"I don't understand," she said.

"Do you expect me to believe that you just happened to walk by that gallery while I happened to be there? This is my life."

She bit her lip and looked past me down the street. "You think that I came looking for you?"

"Yes, I do."

"You must think a lot about yourself." Her English suffered from her anger. "*Tu es très arrogant.* I did not know that you were there. How could I know? I walk this way home from school every day. I thought I was respecting your privacy by walking on." She dropped some euros onto the tray and stood to leave.

I felt like a complete idiot, which was fitting since I was one. "Victoire, I'm sorry."

But she was having none of it, walked past me.

I followed her, walked with her. "Please," I said. "I'm a silly old man and it seems I'm self-centered as well. Please forgive me."

She stopped and turned to face me.

"All of this with us has me on edge, I guess. Running into that woman on the bus. Worrying that I will miss a call from home. I'm not good at this."

"I'm glad you're not good at this," she said. "What would it mean if you were?" She had softened.

"Will you forgive me?" I asked.

She nodded.

There, on the street like that, in plain light, I held her and kissed her. I was surprised and pulled back to discover that she was also.

"You don't have to prove anything," she said.

"I wasn't trying to," I told her. "I just needed to do that. But you're right, I have to be careful."

She reached down and took my hand, held it briefly, then let it go. "There is a rumor that I have tea in my apartment."

House

The Frazars made their deliveries in an old '63 Ford flatbed with a rusted-out quarter panel. I knew this was for the benefit of their so-regarded upscale customers. I had seen the elder Frazar any number of times in his expensive Audi, his very pretty third wife, a former Miss Utah, seated beside him. The boy, Jason, tooled around in a fancy, school-bus-yellow 4x4, the make of which I never knew, but I often wondered if the battery of fog lights actually worked. This to say that they probably had just as much dough as their with-scorn-adjudged clientele and were every bit as ostentatious with said dough, but played a part in the class drama for profit. The irony of course was that it no doubt cost them more to keep their display piece of a truck running than they would have spent on a new truck. If it had been merely an aesthetic choice then I would have been on board, but the deception was fairly barefaced and I found it slightly odious or noisome, as my father might have said.

The truck coughed smoke and banged across my uneven yard to my painting's building. The barrel was strapped to the side wall and the hoses were in a heap beside it. The pump and timer were in a still-sealed box. Jason hopped onto the bed and untied the barrel.

"We only had seven jugs of the caustic soda," Frazar said. "So, you got a fly problem in this building." He regarded the sealed-tight windows. "No flies out here that I can see."

"Like I told Jason, no flies."

"Then why do you need a stable fly suppression system?" he asked.

Jason made a loud noise dropping the barrel onto the ground.

"Careful with that," the father said. He looked back to me.

"In case I should have some flies show up," I said.

"Well, we'll put it in there for you." He started toward the door.

I stepped in front of him, a bit awkwardly. "Actually, you can just leave it out here and I'll take care of it."

He gave me a look that I read as his being offended.

"It's messy in there and I would rather no one go in," I said, feeling a need to explain myself.

He rolled his eyes at his son, a gesture I thought was more for my benefit than anyone else's. "Jason, just put everything over there against the wall." He looked at me. "Okay if we get that close to the building?"

"I have some very private work inside," I said.

"Of course," he said. "Hurry it up, Jason."

Linda pulled up to the house with Will and April. Linda waved. Will never waved; he claimed it was strange gestural behavior that could easily be misconstrued, so he chose not to participate. April waved, a glum look on her face until she saw Jason. Then she smiled warmly.

"Hey, April," Jason called.

"Hi, Jason."

I looked from one to the other, trying to read them. My immediate impression was that there was nothing between them, no secrets, no intrigue. Then I found myself confused by April's sudden brightening; she had been so dour since sharing her news with me.

"Would you two like to come inside for some coffee?" I asked.

The offer caught Frazar off guard. "Well, I don't know."

"Jason here can catch up with April and you can tell me all about the feed business." I must have sounded like a crazy person. I had no idea what I wanted to know about Jason's possible paternity. I didn't know whether I wanted to know or whether it made any difference knowing.

"Jason, you want to talk to April?" Frazar asked his son.

Jason looked at his watch. "No, I got to get back. I have some homework I gotta do."

I was hoping it was English homework, but regardless I again was convinced, however irrationally, that Jason Frazar was the father of my soon-to-be-terminated unformed and unrealized grandchild. I felt no animosity and didn't even feel I needed to blame him; however, I felt suddenly that he had a right to know.

"I wish you would come in," I said, realizing that now I was sounding extremely odd.

"No, I think we'll be going," Frazar said, again with the eye roll.

"Okay," I said. "Come by anytime, Jason."

"C'mon. Let's get out of here, son," Frazar said. He tipped a cap he wasn't wearing to me. "I hope you enjoy your new unit there."

I walked into the house and found April uncharacteristically emptying the dishwasher. Linda and Will were not in the room. I took the utensil rack out and started putting away the flatware.

"Where is everybody?" I asked.

"Mom said she had to call Aunt Jane."

"Will?"

"Who cares?"

"So, Jason was here," I said.

April gave me a look.

"Didn't you go out with him?"

"It's not him," she said. "Why would you think it's Jason?"

"No reason. I knew you'd gone out with him."

She put down the dinner plate she was holding. It teetered on the edge of the counter.

"Watch that plate," I said.

"Do you think I sleep with every boy I go out with?"

"That's not what I meant."

"Why does it matter who it is?" she asked.

"It doesn't," I said.

"Jason Frazar. Oh, please." The *oh, please* she'd learned from her mother and she said it well.

"What's wrong with Jason Frazar?" I asked.

"For one thing, the Frazars are fake poor. They've got more money than anybody but Jason's always throwing that blue-collar bullshit around. He lords the fact he goes to public school over everybody like he's hot shit." That was the most I'd heard April swear. I wondered if our sharing a secret had sanctioned some behavioral changes of which I was unaware.

"Whoever the father is, don't you think he has a right to know?" It was a stupid thing to say, I knew it as I said it, and I imagined then that I must have sounded like I had heard it on television. "Does the boy know?"

"No."

"Isn't there some kind of legal obligation? A father's rights or something? Don't you think it's only fair you tell him?"

Again, "Oh, please." She leaned back, knocked against the teetering plate, and it fell to the floor and broke.

"Give me some credit here. I'm keeping your secret. This is hard." I knelt to pick up the shards.

"Again, who it is doesn't matter," she said.

Linda came into the room. "Who what is?" she asked.

"Nothing," I said.

"A plate broke."

Linda stepped around to see that it was one of the nice dishes. "April," she complained, drawing out the girl's name.

April looked at me and I looked away to the pieces on the floor. "Wasn't her fault," I said.

"I hate this house," April said and walked out.

"Jesus," Linda said. "She's driving me crazy. I'll get the broom." She grabbed the broom from the closet.

"I've got it," I said. I took the broom and the pan from her.

"So, what was that all about?" Linda asked.

"Teenagers," I said.

"What were you talking about?"

"Oh, I mentioned that Jason Frazar had asked about her and somehow that made her mad. Seems like I can't say anything right."

"Yeah." She looked out the window at my shed.

"Something for the painting."

"Will I ever see that thing?" It had been a couple of years since she'd asked about it.

"You know how I feel about the painting."

"I know what you say, but I don't understand it. I feel locked out. In a lot of ways." In fact she was locked out. Literally. *The other ways* was a different discussion, a longer and harder one that I chose not to approach.

"It helps me work. I don't know why, but it does."

"Right."

"Can't there be something in a person's life that is just his? Or hers?"

"Right."

I dumped the pieces from the dustpan into the garbage. "Are you going to be mad for a while?"

"No," she lied. She went to the cupboard. "We have only five of those plates left and Bloomingdale's doesn't carry them anymore."

"Maybe someone else does. Saks?"

"Something's going on with April."

"It's called being sixteen."

"Maybe."

1979

Neither Richard nor I felt much like eating. It was just dusk and we lay beside each other looking at the dead ceiling fan. I assumed he'd drifted off to sleep as I did. We awoke, startled by a loud knock on the door. I looked out the window to see that it was still dark.

"What the fuck?" he said.

I checked my watch. Midnight. The knock, again. I got up and walked to the door. There was no peephole. There was no chain.

"Who is it?" I asked.

"The Bummer."

"Go away," I said.

"Open the fucking door!"

I looked over at Richard. He was up and sitting on the edge of the bed. He shrugged.

"I learned something about the brother," the Bummer said. "Let me in the fucking room."

"Let him in," Richard said.

I opened the door and stepped back into the room. The Bummer leaned in and pointed a finger at Richard, "You, come on, I got somebody who knows something about your brother."

"Yeah, what's he know?" Richard asked.

"Let's go find out."

Richard shook his head and glanced over at me.

"Whatever you want to do," I said.

"We need to go now," the Bummer said.

Richard leaned over and grabbed his shoes.

"I'll be downstairs," the Bummer said. He called back from the hallway, "And bring some money."

"Here we go," I said. I sat in the desk chair to lace up my boots. "Maybe he's got something this time."

Richard didn't say anything.

"We don't have to go with him," I said. "Are you all right?"

"Let's go."

The Bummer didn't speak as he led us six or so blocks to a run-down tavern next to what clearly was a brothel. Women wore bright nothings over their thick thighs and asses, their sagging breasts, stood in huddles and smoked cigarettes and cigars. They eyed us with what might have passed for mild interest then laughed us away. There were no women in the bar. It was not crowded at all. Around a couple of tables sat young men who reminded me of fellow university students from Philadelphia, dressed just slightly better than the establishment. There was a half step down well into the room that I did not see and so landed heavily on my ankle. It might have been sprained, but there was little I could do about it.

"You okay?" Richard asked.

"I think I sprained my ankle." I thought better of asking the bartender for a bag of ice—I didn't need the Bummer's laughter in my face—and then I felt like a macho idiot.

The Bummer fell into a chair at a table where sat a wide-shouldered, mustachioed man. He wore a bright white, pressed T-shirt. His bushy mustache was made more dramatic by the fact that his face was so neatly and expertly shaven everywhere else. He did not have much of a chin. The Bummer gestured with his hand for us to sit and we haltingly did.

"Show him the picture?" the Bummer said to Richard.

"Who are you?" I asked.

The mustache paused to take me in, put out his cigarette in the foil ashtray. The Bummer waved him off and then glared at me and told me to shut up. Richard handed over the photograph.

Mustache stared at the picture for a few seconds. *"He vista a este hombre,"* he said.

"This man is my brother," Richard said, leaning forward, his elbows on the table. *"Mi hermano.* Is he in some kind of trouble?" He looked at the Bummer. "Ask him if he's in trouble."

"He is not in trouble," the mustached man said in English, but with a thick accent. He pulled on his bottle of beer. "Of course, it depends on what you consider to be trouble."

"Where did you see him?" Richard asked. He took back the picture and looked at it himself. "Where?"

The man looked at the Bummer and pulled out a new cigarette. The Bummer nodded to Richard.

"What?" Richard asked.

"I think you're supposed to give him some money," I said.

"Yeah, right." Richard took some bills from his pants pocket and put a ten on the table, pushed it over to the man. If a muscle in the man's face moved I didn't see it. Nothing. Richard put down another ten.

"Are you trying to offend him?" the Bummer asked. "The man has some information that you might want."

"How do I know he's telling the truth?"

"You don't."

Richard turned to me for help, but I could only shrug. I didn't know what to do, didn't know what I would have been doing in his position.

Some young men at another table became loud, rowdy. One stood up and yelled something at the ceiling in Spanish, but I couldn't hear the words. The thin man swayed with drunkenness. Then he saw us.

"Americano!" he shouted.

"That's right, fuckwad!" the Bummer shouted back. In his face I could see that he enjoyed the possibility of a confrontation.

The young Salvadoran took a step toward us, but his friends stopped him, tried to get him to sit down. He pulled away from them, lost his balance, and almost fell over, yet kept his distance.

"Listen, Yankees, our country is not yours," he said in English. Then, *"Vete a la mierda!"*

"Fuck you!" the Bummer shouted back and stood up.

"Are you the CIA?" the man asked. "The fucking CIA is everywhere, come here to fuck us up the ass and take our country."

"We're the kiss my ass," the Bummer said and pulled up the bottom of his shirt to show the butt of his .45.

"CIA," the man said, playing brave, but even I could see that the sight of the weapon frightened him. It frightened me.

"Be cool," I said to the Bummer.

"Shut the fuck up," he said to me.

The men pulled their friend not so easily back to their table and got him back into his chair.

"Fuck you," the Bummer repeated and sat down. He turned his attention to Richard. "Continue," he said in a calm way that was almost comic.

Richard put down another eighty dollars. The man calmly raked the bills together then spoke to the Bummer in Spanish.

"*Él está al otro lado del lago. Los campos al norte de Candelaria. Está con Vargas. Es un corredor.*"

"Fuck," the Bummer said.

"Why *fuck*?" Richard asked. "What's the matter?"

Neither the Bummer nor the mustache responded to Richard. The man stood and shook the Bummer's hand.

"*Gracias*," the Bummer said, hardly looking at him.

To us the man said, with hardly a glance, "*Buena suerte.*" He drained his beer, walked away from the table and toward the door.

"CIA whore!" the thin man at the table of students shouted at the mustache, threw a cardboard coaster at him.

Mustache offered nothing in response, simply left.

"What did he tell you?" Richard asked.

"You brother is in the drugs business. He's mixed up with some Nicaraguans." The Bummer lit a cigarette.

"Did he tell you where he is?"

"You fellows know of course that the shit is about to hit the fan in this fucking country."

"Will you take me to my brother?"

"Or just tell us where he is," I said. To Richard, I stage-whispered, "We don't need this crazy motherfucker."

"Yeah, I'll take you to him," Bummer said. "It's fucking dangerous out there. I want you to know that."

"Okay, okay," Richard said. "Take me to my brother. When do we leave?"

"Now."

Paris

Perhaps it was my pathetic accusation and an accompanying need to blot out my hurtful behavior or perhaps it was simply that we knew each other better that second time, but our sex was more vigorous and still just as sweet and open as the first time. Her hands caressed me with a certainty that was at once comforting and bewildering, and I felt that I touched her in much the same way. Like the first time, I was struck by my lack of guilt. Part of it was that I understood that I had chosen to be there with Victoire and so feeling guilt would have been not only disingenuous, but mere show, and for whom? But of course this lack of guilt about what I was doing with this woman with whom I clearly saw no future left me with, well, guilt. I felt guilt for feeling no guilt. I lay there with her head on my chest thinking there should be a term for this guilty guiltlessness. If this feeling were a color, I considered, it would be the orange threads of slightly diluted saffron.

Victoire suddenly sat up in bed and told me she had something special for me to see.

"And what might that be?" I asked.

"You will see." She got me out of bed and led me naked to the center of the room. She grabbed a chair from the dining table and put it in the middle of the room, positioned to face the wall opposite the window.

"What is all of this?" I asked.

"Sit," she said.

I did. The wood was cool against my ass. I liked the sensation.

"Close your eyes. Please don't look."

"My eyes are shut."

I heard her move around the room, but I kept my eyes closed. She told me I could open them and I did. Against the wall pinned to a foam-core board that leaned against the wall was a watercolor. The paper was about twenty by thirty inches. The work was green, green leaning into blue in places, edged with blood in the southeast corner. It was abstract, stunning. It was so unlike the country scenes and cityscapes of hers that I had seen before. The painting was rich, dense, and deep. Too deep, I thought, for a work on paper, no matter how heavy the stock, too rich to be anything but oil colors, but it was surely watercolors. I was surprised by it, confused by it. I began to cry.

"Do you like it?"

"Did you make this?" I asked.

"You think a young, pretty French girl cannot paint this picture?"

"I don't believe anyone could make this picture. How did you do it?" I wanted to get up and walk over to it, to get right up on it, but I also did not want to end the experience I was having with it. "I love it."

Even if I had decided to get up I couldn't have because Victoire threw a naked leg over me and straddled me. It was only after she had guided me inside her that I realized the painting aroused me. We rocked there in that little chair, her back to the painting, my eyes on it.

"I want you to come inside me," she said. "I know you cannot, but I would like you to." It was right then that I realized that I was not wearing a condom. I did not stop. She felt perfect.

"I call it *Verdant*," she whispered.

"Perfect," I said. And it was, the title suggesting a landscape that was not there and the color that was complex and yet just simply that. In the painting I saw Victoire and understood why I was with her.

I wanted to go to sleep and awake properly, light from a window striking my face, the songs of birds, the sounds of a garbage truck. That was what I did, that was how I awoke, and it felt right until I realized that I was not in my hotel, not near the hotel phone, but beside Victoire in her bed.

I managed to leave that bed and the apartment without disturbing Victoire too much. She knew I was leaving and she might have even said good-bye or blown me a kiss. Instead of catching the metro near her place I walked all the way up to Saint-Germain and then west to the Odéon. It was half past eight, which meant it was two thirty in the morning at home. I took the 10 line to Sèvres-Babylone and walked to my hotel. On my way I passed the elaborate Christmas decorations in the windows of Le Bon Marché. They were full of moving parts that were shut down at this hour and they seemed like some kind of metaphor.

I stepped into the overheated lobby of my hotel and peeled off my scarf as the clerk handed me my key. He also handed me a folded pink paper. I stared at the paper in my hand.

"Your wife," the very neat man said in English.

"What time did she call?" I asked.

"I remember it was around five this morning, but the message says exactly." He didn't look at my eyes.

"*Merci.*" I slipped the paper into my coat pocket without reading it. I took the stairs to my floor because I didn't want to stand in view of the clerk waiting for the elevator.

Once I was in my room I took off my coat, retrieved the message from my pocket, and sat on the edge of the bed. I looked at the phone and jumped when it rang. I let it ring another time then picked up.

"Monsieur Pace? This is Pierre from the front desk."

"*Oui?*"

"I neglected to tell you that I did not tell your wife that you were out, only that you were not answering."

"*Merci, Pierre.*" I hung up. I had conveniently managed to talk myself out of feeling guilt, but now with the unsolicited complicity of Pierre, I could not maintain my delusion.

I took my calling card from my wallet and stared at it, flipped it through my fingers like a playing card. I thought of calling home and then remembered it was three in the morning there. If it had been an emergency Linda would have called more than once. Pierre, in his tight-fitting vest two shades lighter than his suit, had saved my pathetic ass, whether he knew so or not; he knew. I entertained the notion of buying him a bottle of wine, but that seemed not only an admission of guilt, but guilt of something unseemly, perhaps dirty. And though I felt bad, I also felt good and none of what I quite properly had to feel guilty about was to me in any way unseemly. In fact, I felt more myself than I had in some years and I didn't even know what that meant.

I left the room at eleven to find a croissant, which was not difficult. One could not throw a stick and not hit a patisserie. On the other hand, there was no finding a cup of coffee to go, so I sat at an outdoor table of a café a couple of doors away and had a coffee while I ate a *pain au chocolat* from the bakery across the street. At noon I returned to the hotel then waited another hour before calling home.

Linda answered.

"Good morning," I said. "Sorry I missed your call. The clerk just delivered the message to me a couple of hours ago. He was very apologetic. He thinks he rang the wrong room."

"It's snowing," she said.

"Really?"

"Quite heavily."

"I'll be home in just a week."

"Where is the good snow shovel? The new one."

I could see the shovel in my head, blue blade, white handle. "It's in the garage with the old one, beside April's old tricycle."

"Okay."

"Linda, is everything okay?"

"You tell me," she said.

"I'll be home in four days," I said.

"They're thinking about closing the schools. What am I supposed to do with these guys?"

"Call Beth." Beth was our part-time nanny who preferred the term *babysitter.* "Give her some extra hours. That's why we have her."

"Do you know how much that will cost?"

"Cheaper than a therapist," I said.

I could hear an almost smile and just as quickly its evaporation. "Well, I'd better get breakfast started."

"The gallery looks good," I said.

"Good."

"I'll call you later," I said.

I hung up and fell back onto the bed, stared up at the ceiling. My chest was tight. I couldn't seem to pull in a satisfactory breath.

House

Which of my offspring would I sacrifice? I had to test my method of destruction.

I chose a painting that had been wanted by a couple from Cleveland, but to whom I had decided not to sell. They were confused by my refusal of their money, finally claiming to feel wounded, indignant, choosing to think I had decided that they were not worthy of the work. They would not believe that I was unhappy with the painting itself, even after I offered a similar, and I thought better, painting for considerably less money. It was a smallish canvas, more geometric in composition than most of my work, a wide palate depleting itself as it moved from northwest southeast. I took the canvas into the private shed and locked myself in, put on my mask and heavy gloves, filled a spray bottle with caustic soda, and attacked the work. The chemical foamed ever so slightly but mostly ran down the surface and fell onto the tarp below. I stood back to see how well I had ruined the work and was surprised and disappointed to watch the painting become actually more interesting. Truth be told, my feelings were just a bit injured by the fact that I had made the work better by trying to destroy it. The colors, which had always been too close to primary for me, became richer for their distress, blended more interestingly. More disappointing was that my plan for automated destruction had to be abandoned. I still had no way to control the life—rather, death—of the painting. I lifted my dust mask and sat in the only seat in the barn, an old wooden swiveling desk chair, and stared at the enormous canvas, wondered what kind of selfish need I was attempting to satisfy. Regardless, selfish or no, childish or no, the need was real. The painting was mine, only mine, I wanted it to be only mine, to mean for me and for me alone. I also wondered why I was making it. The painting was supposed to help me understand something, maybe connect with the world that I did not so much like, but as I sat there considering my current dilemma, it offered me nothing at all. Abstract as it was, it was essentially a time line, simple as that, but time didn't move along it, there were no intervals, nothing changed, accelerated, or stopped. The fact that it was secret served its secrets, my secrets, and suddenly I understood at least one rather simple and perhaps obvious forehead-flattening truth, that a secret can exist only if its revelation, discovery, even betrayal is possible.

My nights were less peppered with the bad dreams, but the memory of them haunted me as much as they ever did and did so while I was awake. The recollection of the dreams became a thing and the painting became the place I put the pieces of that thing.

A knock. It was Richard. I knew because he shouted, "It's me, Richard! Or is it: It is I, Richard! *I* is probably correct but I'd sound like such a wanker saying it. Of course I sound like a wanker saying *wanker.*"

I stepped outside and joined him.

"You really are not going to let me ever see that thing, are you?" he said.

"Nope."

"What's with all this tubing?" he asked.

"It's a stable fly suppression apparatus."

"You've got a fly problem?"

"It's a waste of money is what it is," I said. "What's up?"

"Nothing. Just came to check on you."

"You could have just called."

He raised one eyebrow and looked at me. I never answered the phone and hardly ever responded to messages, not out of grumpiness or disrespect, but because of a bad memory.

"I'm okay."

"What about April?"

"Let's go to the other studio." We talked as we walked across the property. "I was thinking."

"Always a bad thing."

"Why is it okay that I told you? I've already broken her secret."

"Betrayed her secret," Richard corrected me. "You break a promise. Are you a native speaker?"

"Right. You know what I mean."

"But she doesn't know that you told me," Richard said. "If she knew, she'd be pissed."

"So, why can't I tell Linda and Linda won't tell April that I told her and then Linda would know the way she's supposed to know?"

We stepped into the studio and I switched on the lights. So many paintings. So much work. So much time.

Richard laughed softly. "How long would that last? April would know that Linda knew as soon as she looked at her. Maybe you should talk to a shrink."

"What for? I don't need to explore why I made such a fucked-up promise in the first place. I made it and now I have to deal with it."

"Linda doesn't have to know everything. Just throwing that out there. She doesn't know everything about you."

"This is different. This is her daughter. Plus, I don't think I'm helping April all that much. I believe she needs to talk to her mother. I mean, all I do is say *okay* and *whatever you want*. Should I have gotten mad and yelled at her?"

"No."

I moved a couple of small canvases across the room.

"Do you remember Abbey Lincoln?"

"The singer?"

"Yes. We went to hear her when we were in graduate school."

"I remember. She was in that movie." I couldn't come up with the title. "Why do you ask?"

"She died last year. I thought I saw her the other day, but then I realized that it couldn't be her, because the woman I saw looked like she looked in nineteen seventy-eight. Anyway, she died. She was eighty."

"Wow. We're old men. We heard her at the Village Vanguard. I remember that pretty clearly."

"We should go back there," Richard said.

"It's not the same anymore," I said. "Hearing jazz, I mean. People just sit around like they're in church, a white church. No offense."

"None taken." Richard looked out the window at the house. "Still, live music sounds good, doesn't it? Maybe you should take April out to hear some live jazz. Father-daughter stuff."

I looked over at my good friend. "Thanks," I said.

"There are all these young people playing jazz now. She might like some of them."

"Hungry?" I asked. "I'm about to go in and start dinner."

"No, I'm fine." He paused and looked at me. "You had a crush on Abbey Lincoln."

"No, *you* had the crush on Abbey Lincoln."

"You're right. Too late now."

1979

We walked out of the bar and into the street. It had rained while we were inside and everything was wet and shiny. The Bummer pumped up his chest and smiled at some hookers next door.

"I think I'll take my money now," the Bummer said.

"You said after you found him," Richard said.

"We're almost there. Give me the money."

Richard gave me an exasperated look.

"I really don't see any point in arguing with him," I said. "It's just money and he's going to get it anyway."

The Bummer laughed at me. "Just money," he repeated. "Rich college boy. Just money."

Richard reached down and pulled the money from his boot.

"You know, Spanky," the Bummer said, "that's the first place the bad people will look for dough on a dead man." He accepted the money and put it in his jacket pocket without counting.

"So, let's go," Richard said.

"First, I'm going to get my knob polished," the Bummer said. "If I were you I'd do the same thing. We might get wet out there and it's good to be loose, relaxed. Know what I mean?" With that he walked toward the hookers. "Meet you back here in ten," he called to us.

"Knob polished," I said. "Who really says that?"

"He does."

"What does that even mean? I don't have a knob on my dick. Do you have a knob on your dick? I hate this guy."

"So, what do we do?" Richard asked.

"I guess we stand here like the idiots we are until he's done with his knob polishing."

I looked up and down the street. Far off there was singing or chanting, then sirens. Some of the students from the bar came out and walked with deliberation toward the commotion.

"This place is a mess," Richard said. "I just want to get the fuck out of here before everything goes to hell."

"You got that right."

A truckload of soldiers drove by us. The scared-looking young men seated in the uncovered back stared at us and we tried to not make eye contact. "Where is that motherfucker?" Richard looked at his watch. "It's already one thirty. I hate my fucking brother."

"Me too."

"What I really want to do right now is get drunk."

"Me too."

The Bummer returned, shaking his pant leg, grumbling and half laughing. "How much of an IQ does it take to suck a goddamn cock?" he said.

"You tell me," I said.

He passed over my remark while managing to cut me a glance. "If you girls don't mind I thought we'd use the Caddy again."

"Of course," Richard said. "Why the fuck not?"

"I'm detecting an attitude," the Bummer said.

"And he's also a great reader of people," Richard said. "We'll need to get some gas."

"Already done," the Bummer said. When Richard gave him a puzzled look, "I'm a professional, boy."

"Aren't you going to need your big gun?" I asked.

"I left it with the desk clerk at your hotel," he said. "He was very accommodating."

"I'll bet," I said.

As we walked back, the street became more active. Small clusters of people, mostly young men, walked quickly or ran in every direction, it seemed. A couple more trucks of soldiers rolled by, each batch of men looking younger and more frightened. A panel van with a public address system passed us, a voice blaring, *"Todo adentro por orden del alcalde!"*

"What did he say?" I asked Richard.

The Bummer answered, "They want everybody inside. It's good we're clearing out of town. Gonna be a party."

At the hotel Richard went up to the room to use the toilet. I sat in an oversized chair in the lobby, watched while the Bummer retrieved his weapon from the properly scared-to-death desk clerk. He took a magazine from his jacket, tapped it against the counter, and snapped it into the rifle while staring the clerk in the face. He nodded to the man before turning away. He smiled as he walked back toward me. "Without ammo this thing is just a boat paddle," he said.

"Okay."

He sat on the arm of a sofa and looked out the window at the people passing by. "Messy, very messy," he said. "So, how did your buddy talk you into coming down here?"

It wasn't that I had no answer for him, but I was startled by the almost normal-sounding question.

"I mean, all the way the fuck down here for his fuckup brother? Really, who does that?"

I looked the Bummer in the eye. "He's my friend."

For the briefest second I at least imagined that I saw a flicker of respect for me, but he said, "Fucking dumbshit."

I shrugged; that was true enough. "Why are you here?"

Richard was just coming down the stairs.

The Bummer was not looking at me when he said, "Because I'm a fucking war criminal. Can't go back to the States. And I like to kill people, shoot them, anyway."

"I'm ready," Richard said.

"Your makeup looks nice," the Bummer said to Richard.

"Fuck you."

"Let's go, girlies. Let's blow this pop stand before the walls cave in. I've always loved that saying. I don't get it, but I like it. What the fuck is a pop stand? And why would the wall cave in?"

The drive out of town proved to be complicated and difficult. At a couple of intersections we had to detour to avoid crowds in the street. Strangely, fortunately, the soldiers both on foot and in jeeps showed no appreciable interest in us, in our lumbering Cadillac. Regardless, I was more than less terrified, as was Richard. If the Bummer was concerned at all he didn't show it. Richard was driving at the insistence of the Bummer and so I was in the backseat (where I belonged, our asshole guide having said as much outright). Otherwise I was fairly ignored while the Bummer conducted our circuitous route out of the city. Finally the traffic trimmed, pedestrian and automotive, as we cleared the city center. My fear had worked its way into numbness, the kind that verged on burning pain. I felt surprisingly unalarmed at the sight of a car that had been set afire, perhaps because there were so few people around. Hindsight suggests that I should have been more nervous for this lack. We drove west through the poor and dark and seemingly quiet suburbs. It was well after two in the morning when we drove past the airport. Richard looked at me in the mirror and we shared the same thought, a desire to abandon this and board a plane for anywhere else. The Bummer switched on the radio. The reception was scratchy, faded in and out, and there were only voices, no music, no ads, only excited Salvadoran Spanish, sentences that never seemed to be completed before another speaker began.

"Do you work for the CIA?" I asked the Bummer.

"What is this CIA?" he asked. I could hear him smiling. "You sound like that punk in the bar."

"No, really," I said, "is that why you're here in El Salvador?" In my mind he was certainly a terrorizing, destabilizing devil.

"No, sweetheart, I don't work for the fucking CIA."

"Then why are you here?" I asked.

"Everybody's got to be someplace. Where are you boys from again? Yeah, Philadelphia. Why do you live there? You could be living in Oregon or Miami. You gotta live somewhere."

Neither Richard nor I said anything to this.

"I used to like this place," the Bummer said. "The winters here are very nice."

I laughed out loud.

"What?" the Bummer asked.

"Fuck you," I said.

Now the Bummer laughed. "Stay on Highway One," he said to Richard. "One or One West."

I looked at Richard's profile. "Are you tired?" I asked him. "Want me to drive for a while?"

"He's fine," the Bummer said.

"I'm asking him," I said.

"Look who found his Y chromosome."

"I'm okay," Richard said.

I looked out the window and saw the new moon break through the clouds. We rolled on for a while. The Cadillac was suffering, missing, taking the hills with difficulty. It was just becoming light when the Bummer instructed Richard to turn south off the highway. The road ran down along a ridge between arroyos. The moon ducked into the clouds again and then fog rolled in and it was all very dark. I could see Richard struggling to stay awake.

"Richard, pull over and let me drive," I said.

Richard look over at the Bummer.

"Pull over," I repeated.

"He wants to drive, let him drive," the Bummer said.

Richard stopped the car. I got out on the passenger side, squeezing by the barely leaning forward Bummer, and discovered that in the darkness Richard had pulled over and stopped only feet from a precipitous drop down into a foggy nothing. I walked around the car and met him at the back of the car.

"You might want to stop here," I said.

"What?"

"Pretty close to a cliff."

We stood there and urinated.

"You know, this whole thing is not getting even a little bit sweeter," I said. I sighed in an effort to relax.

"Let's just get Tad and go home. You think this guy is just fucking with us?"

"Who knows," I said. "Yes, of course he's fucking with us, but maybe he's really taking us to your brother. All I know is that I'm glad to be out of that city."

"Me too," Richard said. "At least the airport's on this side of town. We get Tad and then it's straight to the airport and we'll wait there however long it takes."

"Our bags," Richard said.

"Fuck our bags."

The Bummer called from the car, "If you girls are finished kissing, maybe we can go."

Paris

I woke alone in my hotel room, a room that had become oddly strange, where I wandered to late at night only to sleep. The bed was too soft and left my lower back feeling weak and uncertain. The bedside telephone, an old-fashioned princess, had remained quiet all night; Linda had not called. I had the sad happy feeling of missing my children. It was Will's practice, at two years old, to come to my bedside just before sunup every day and ask to be let under the covers. It had become automatic for me to lift up the quilt and sheet for him to slide into bed next to me. It was a ritual that I knew would not continue forever and so I was determined to enjoy it for as long as it lasted. This morning, being so far away, I missed it. And I missed doing homework with April, a pretend struggle for her mainly because it bored her. I thought of the snow and of playing in it with them, but I rationalized my being away from them by reason of work, the gallery. Though technically true, the lie stuck in my unconscious throat. However, I was anything but truly sad. I was floating like the stupid old man I was, eager to see my reason for remaining happily in Paris.

Sex with Victoire was intense enough, but not what I might have dreamed of if I had had the forethought to dream such things. I had tried to avoid comparison of the young woman with my wife, found the idea distasteful and in bad form, but I did compare them and only to come to the realization that the comparison didn't matter, was without substance. Familiarity with Linda had, quite naturally, yielded a routine, but it was and continued to be satisfying, if infrequent, and that was perhaps more my fault more than hers. But sex with Victoire, whereas it was not unsatisfying, was not so electric, however sweet and charmingly clumsy it might have been.

It was this truth that made the situation with Victoire that much scarier. I was not there in her bed night after night because I was having unbelievable sex. I was there because I wanted to be with her specifically, because in fact I enjoyed trying to please her. It was all so beautifully, awkwardly, painfully intimate.

"What are you thinking about?" Victoire asked.

We had just sat down on a damp bench in a little park from which we could look across the Seine at Notre-Dame Cathedral. We had bought a croissant that we now shared. The bread shattered into a rain of crumbs as I broke it in two.

"There is no neat way to eat a good croissant," she said. She used the back of her hand to brush the flakes of the pastry off my jacket. "The crumbs seem dry, but they are full of butter. So, what is troubling you?"

"Nothing," I said.

"But you're so quiet. More quiet than usual."

"Why are you here with me?" I asked.

"*Pardon?*"

"Victoire, you are a beautiful young woman. Men are drawn to you. Men your age. I'm an old married man. I have two children. I live in another country. I can offer you nothing."

"That's not true," she said.

"How is any of that not true?"

"First of all, I don't want anything from you. Except you."

"That's my point. You can't have me," I said. "I'm not going to leave my wife and children."

"But I do have you, don't I? You are right here beside me, eating the same croissant, looking at the same overstated church. We lie in the same bed, breathe the same air."

I nodded. "I have a family."

"I love you."

"What?"

"*Je t'aime.*"

I said nothing to this.

"I know that you love me, too," she said. "You don't have to say it. I know that it is true."

"How do you know that?"

"I know. It is in the way you look at me. The way you touch me. Don't you love me?"

I looked across the park at a couple of young boys busy on the small playground apparatus. I didn't answer her. I was silent not because she would not like the answer, but because I would not.

"Anyway, I know you love me."

"Suppose," I said, "we were together. Just for the sake of argument, imagine it. I will die long before you."

"And then I will be sad before having a happy rest of my life. I will find another man. Maybe another old man like you. Maybe a younger one."

Her answer was so clean, so perfect, so smart. "Of course," I said. I reached over and held her hand.

"I told you. You do love me. *Tu es mon beau ténébreux.*" She leaned over and placed her head against my shoulder. It was an agreeable feeling, a nice weight. I would later confess to myself, sadly, that everything she had said I wanted to hear. I studied the top of her beautiful twenty-two-year-old head, peered through her hair, through her unblemished scalp, through her bone and into her brain, and loved her, wanted her to feel loved. More precisely, I wanted her to feel loved by me. It sounded as stupid then as it does now.

"Still, it might appear to some that this old man is taking advantage of you," I said.

"This is France."

"It doesn't matter. Would you tell your mother about me?" I knew nothing of her relationship with her mother, but I considered it a reasonable question.

"I have," she said.

"You've done what?"

"She would like to meet you."

"She knows I'm married?"

"She knows everything."

"I see. And this is okay with her? Her daughter having an affair with a married man nearly twenty-five years older. And she knows I have young children?" I didn't care if French people or American people or any people might be troubled by our situation, relationship, it sounded plenty horrible to me. "What about your father? Does he know also?"

"No," she said. "I don't think he would be happy about us. In fact I know that he would not like it."

"That's because he's a reasonable person." Hearing this frightened me slightly, but was also quite oddly reassuring or heartening, though I was not certain why. "So, he doesn't know."

She nodded.

"Doesn't that suggest that you see there's something wrong here, the fact that you won't tell your father?"

"My father is too protective."

"That's his job," I said.

All of this with her head resting gently on my shoulder. She closed the subject with a well-aimed *"Je t'aime."*

"After this will you go into Shakespeare and Company with me?" I asked. "It's just behind us."

"If you like. Are you looking for anything in particular?"

"I'm looking for some books for April and Will, something to take home to them." I said their names to make them more real for her.

"You should take them something French," she said.

"You mean like little Eiffel Towers? Berets?"

"What about a young French stepmother?" She glanced up to examine the look on my face.

I laughed and she laughed harder.

She nestled her head back into my shoulder. *"Je t'aime."*

"Je t'aime, aussi."

"I knew it," she said.

House

Will had come to me, rather uncharacteristically, baseball in hand, and asked me to play catch. He had never liked sports of any kind, except for swimming, and, as far as I knew, he hated balls of any kind. Now at twelve he had grabbed the dusty gloves from the shelves in the garage and wanted to stand out in the yard with me and throw the ball back and forth. He was understandably awkward for a while, but he began to get the hang of it. He was stiff with the glove, while I was a bit self-conscious and unquiet in my interaction with him.

"So, why the gloves and ball?" I asked.

"I just want to be better at it."

"New girlfriend who's a ballplayer?"

"Naw. Just feel like throwing."

"Everything okay at school?"

"Yeah." Will tossed the ball back to me and glanced back at the house. "Is April all right?"

"Why do you ask?"

"She's so mad all the time," he said.

"So, what's different?"

"She's just not the same. She doesn't care about trying to piss me off. She just seems kind of different, you know?"

I nodded. "I'm sure she's fine. Tell you what, I'll talk to her." I didn't want to undermine his confidence. "You're right, though, something's different."

He looked sad.

"I don't think you should worry."

He tossed a ball wildly past me, apologized.

I retrieved it and tossed a pop fly back to him. "I'm sorry I've been sort of absent lately."

Will laughed a little.

"What?"

"You're always absent." He didn't mean it in a critical way, I felt that. "You're just always in your head. That's what Mom says anyway. And I get it. You're an artist; you need to be in there."

"You get it, eh? Well, your mother is just being generous. I need to be better," I said. "Anything going on at school that I should know about? Swim meet or something? Drug deals?"

"Meets haven't started yet. Just practices. The drug deals are all next semester, but they're a cinch."

"I wish I could swim like you. I'm a stone in the water."

"Yeah, I know."

We tossed for a while longer without talking. I was impressed with my son, having shown the initiative to find me and ask about his sister, showing the concern he did.

What was clear now was that if Will had noticed his sister's change then certainly Linda had noticed as well. I now not only realized how deep I was into this mess but I could feel the walls beginning to crumble and cave in. I would have to tell Linda that night and April would have to live with the fact that her father was an unreliable lying bastard.

That night at dinner April was particularly testy. Her mother, who kept up with such things as school projects and the like, asked about some history assignment, to which April responded, "It's not your assignment, so why do you care?"

"I take it that means you haven't started it."

"Why don't you do it then?"

Linda looked at me as if for help.

"Your mother's just trying to be helpful," I said.

"Right. *Helpful* is synonymous with *controlling*."

I could see how uncomfortable this was making Will, so I tried to change the mood at the table. "Will and I actually played catch today. Gloves and everything."

Linda smiled at Will.

"Whoop-de-do," April said. Then she leaned slightly forward with a grimace that I believed only I saw.

I looked at her eyes, tried to telepathically ask her what was wrong. Her eyes teared up. The wet eyes were noticed by Linda.

"What is it?" Linda asked.

"I feel sick," April said. "May I leave the table?"

"Of course, honey," Linda said.

As April stood, her balance abandoned her for a second and she fell back down into her chair.

"April?" Linda said.

"Just my back."

"Did you hurt it today?"

April left the table and disappeared down the hall.

Linda looked at me and mouthed the words, "Period maybe."

I nodded.

Then she said, I imagine for Will's benefit, "She's wound rather tightly these days, isn't she?"

"You think," Will said.

"We should give her some space," I said.

Linda cut me a glance that frankly frightened me.

"What?"

"Nothing," she said.

Nothing meant shut the fuck up and so I did just that. Will and I cleared the table and Linda went to check on April.

"Well, that was fun," Will said. He dumped the last of the salad into the can and handed me the bowl and tossers. "What did you think you were going to be when you were my age?"

"That's a good question," I said.

"That's what people usually say when they don't know or if they're simply about to lie."

"I do remember wanting to be a pilot, but I can't remember if I was four or fourteen. Maybe I was forty."

"A pilot? You mean like jets? Did they have jets back then?"

"They had jets, smart-ass. I had an uncle who was in World War II and he was a pilot. He was one of those Tuskegee Airmen and he was sort of well known, I think. Not famous. He was my mother's brother and she adored him."

"So, you stopped wanting to be a pilot?"

"Well, I finally met the uncle. Uncle Ty."

"And?"

"Uncle Ty was a fucking asshole."

Will laughed the way kids laugh when a parent swears.

"He was a drunk and he only ever thought about himself." As I said this I wondered how I really differed from Uncle Ty. I had stopped drinking, but in my mind I was still a drunk. "He drove his new convertible into a sewage treatment pond and drowned."

Will laughed. "He drowned in poo?"

"Drowned in poo."

Linda joined us in the kitchen, not angry but annoyed. "Well, it seems April needs her space." Will was still chuckling about the asshole uncle and Linda noticed. "What's so funny?"

"Nothing," Will said.

Linda gave me another unhappy look.

"Has April said anything to you, Will?"

"She told me to fuck myself," he said.

"Language," Linda said.

1979

I had just gotten behind the wheel and pulled away from the shoulder when the sky began to lighten. Another hour on the rough road brought us to a small collection of shacks. At an intersection there was a sign for Iglesia La Luz Mundo. I liked the irony at least.

"Which way?" I asked the Bummer.

He snapped to, apparently having drifted off to sleep. He seemed embarrassed by this as he gathered himself and got his bearings. He rubbed his fists into his eyes. "Just stay on this road. We should see the lake pretty soon here."

"I need to eat," I said. I didn't want to eat, but I did in fact need fuel. I also needed to be out of that tight, enclosed space, needed air, some distance from the Bummer. I needed a time-out.

"You're shitting me," the Bummer said.

"No, I'm not," I said, calmly.

"I'm hungry, too," from Richard in the backseat.

"You see a place, you pull over." The Bummer shook his head and threw up his hand in a gesture of helplessness. "Hungry," he said, just under his breath. Then, louder, "Fucking pussies."

The lake came into sight below us. It was large, maybe beautiful, desolate. If it is possible for a lake full of water to appear dry, then this one did. A short distance after the dirt trail turned left to follow the shoreline there was a cantina, not so different looking from the one in the mountains, except one of the cinder-block walls was actually unfinished. Beside the open front door was a fire pit over which a goat was skewered, the coals cadmium red, the carcass black.

"It's awfully early," Richard said.

"Door's open," the Bummer said.

Richard pointed down the hill. "Fishermen down there. Probably open early for them."

"Let's find out," I said.

The Bummer was already out of the car. He walked over to the goat and ripped off a bit of meat. He chewed it and wiped his mouth with his sleeve. He made a show of working his jaw. "They can slow roast this motherfucker for a week and it'll still be tougher than a dog's tit."

Richard looked at me. "What the fuck?"

"Hillbilly talk," I said.

We ducked in through the short doorway. There were four tables set up on plywood subflooring. A short, round elderly woman with a beautifully wrinkled brown face gestured for us to sit wherever we liked. The hard ladder-backed chairs were a welcome change from the beaten-down seats of the Caddy.

The woman came to our table. *"Quieres comer?"*

"Sí," I said. *"Por favor."*

"Cerveza," the Bummer said.

"No cerveza," she said.

"What?" the Bummer said.

"Huevos picados, plátanos fritos, pupusas." She looked at me and Richard, but avoided the Bummer.

"Huevos picados," Richard said.

"Mismo," I said.

"Cerveza," the Bummer said again.

The woman shook her head. *"No cerveza."*

"Bring some fucking eggs. *Huevos.*" The Bummer watched her walk away into the kitchen. "Lying bitch."

"Be cool," I said.

"I know for a fucking fact she's got beer back there." But he didn't get up to check.

"So, what's the story with the Nicaraguans?" Richard asked.

"They think they're badass drug runners," the Bummer said.

"They run their shit through El Salvador because it's too hot down south. That's changing, though. I'm not sure how the fuck they do it. Ruthless motherfuckers. They would just as soon shoot you as look at you."

"Do you know any of them?" Richard asked.

"I've seen them," he said. He looked at us. "You scared?"

"You're fucking right I'm scared," I told him.

"Well, hold it together so you don't fuck the shit up."

"Fuck the shit up?" Richard said. "Fuck the shit up? What are you talking about? The shit, as you call it, is already fucked up. What is the shit anyway? Everything is fucked up."

"Same goes for you," the Bummer said and pointed his middle finger at Richard. "You two just do what I say when I fucking say do it. No questions, no hesitation, just do it."

I thought about talking to the Bummer, asking him if he got off on all of this, but I didn't care anymore. I quite simply wanted all of it to be over. I didn't even care if Richard got his brother back anymore, and a part of me hoped we wouldn't find him. I looked at the gray walls of the cantina, at the staggered grid of the cinder blocks. There was a crucifix on the far wall. Poor Jesus.

We had not seen a car, truck, or bus on the way down to the lake, but the sound of a vehicle sliding to a stop found us. I thought it was probably soldiers. It turned out to be two armed men, but not military, not government military anyway, and with them was Carlos, the Dutch man from the mountains.

"Look who we have here," Carlos said.

The two other men sat at the table farthest from us and Carlos came and sat with us. Again he had his notebook with him. This time he also had a Polaroid camera draped over his shoulder. He didn't offer his hand to shake, didn't look at Richard, but nodded to me.

"Where are you lads headed?" Carlos asked. "Still out looking for the lost brother?"

"Still looking," the Bummer said.

"Who are your friends?" I asked.

"I'm not sure," Carlos said. "Either the Partido Revolucionario de los Trabajadores Centroamericanos or the Partido Comunista Salvadoreño." He enjoyed the Spanish. "It's like music, isn't it? Or maybe they're just two guys with guns. Who the fuck knows? Who the fuck cares?"

I stared at the notebook and Carlos caught me.

"You really want to see what's in here, don't you?" he said. He stroked the cover with his fingers.

I nodded.

He pushed it over to me. "Go ahead, take a look."

I opened the notebook. It was filled with plastic sleeves with four Polaroid pictures per page. Each photograph was of a face. I couldn't look away. I turned six pages and then looked at Richard.

"What is it?" Richard said.

I looked at Carlos. "Are these dead people?"

"I prefer to think of them as the dearly departed."

"Why do you have pictures of dead people?" I pushed the book toward Richard so that he could see.

"Just because a person is dead doesn't mean he's worthless." Carlos put a cigarette in his mouth. He offered one to me and I refused. The Bummer and Richard accepted.

"I don't understand," I said.

"My boy, there is a nasty war going on in this little country. People go missing all the time. Loved ones worry, loved ones wonder. I address that need. And loved ones pay."

"People pay you to look at this book?" I asked.

Carlos looked back at the kitchen. "I could use some food. Smells good, whatever it is."

"You charge people money to look at these pictures," I said.

"It's a living." He heard his own words, laughed. "So to speak." Perhaps it was that man's face, perhaps it was the fatigue, perhaps it was everything piling up without promise of relief, perhaps it was the memory of that little girl and the secret shared by Luis and me, but I wanted to leap across that table and tear out that man's throat.

The Bummer must have seen it come over me and I think it even unsettled him a bit, a least to the extent that he didn't want any trouble. He said, "What's taking so long with that food? *Mamacita!*"

Richard knew I was on the edge. "We'll find Tad and then we'll be on our way home."

I stared at Carlos for a few awkward seconds. "Fuck you," I said. I stood up and walked outside.

I sat on the hood of the Caddy. It was full light now. The lake was plain to see. I could just barely make out the far side of it. Richard came out with his plate and mine. He handed me a fork.

"Thanks," I said.

"Tad and then we go," he said.

I nodded.

"Are you okay?"

"I want to kill that man," I said.

"I can tell."

"I'm not a violent person."

"I know," Richard said.

I thought about telling Richard about the little boy and his sister's hand, but I could not bring myself to do it. "We came to this country and dug a grave," I said. "A fucking grave, Richard."

"Yeah."

"What the fuck, man?"

"We'll just get Tad and go."

"Both of those motherfuckers are crazy. We're going to die here, you know that, don't you?"

"No, we're not," Richard said.

"I don't want to die in this fucking place. This is the first lake I've ever seen that I don't like."

Richard looked at the water. "We'll get home."

I could see his fear. I was actually speaking out of anger. I realized that that emotion was suppressing my fear. Looking at Richard, I became determined to make it back home, even if it was Baltimore Avenue in Philadelphia.

"Food's not bad," Richard said.

I tasted it. It was good. "Not bad," I said.

"Tad and go. That will be our mantra," Richard said.

"You got it."

"What color would you call that?" Richard pointed at the sky.

"I would call that a very light manganese blue," I said.

Paris

The rain became white noise, but I remained awake. I recalled how Will had needed white noise to put him to sleep, a machine that sounded a little like rain or static or a muffled heartbeat. Even the sound of the rain outside now itself was not the rain; it was a mere abstraction of the rain. I closed my eyes and saw a painting, a large painting. I saw it completely for just a second and then it was gone, a mere memory. Against all logic the painting was not abstract, as it was not drawn out of or away from form, from nature. When I awoke I would tell myself my dreams and those tellings would be abstractions, but that painting, that painting was real, real color, real shape, texture, light, and shadow.

The rain wouldn't let up. I sat on the bed of my hotel room looking down at rue Saint-Placide. A block away was Le Bon Marché and I thought about what I might find in there for the children and Linda. But really I was waiting for the rain to let up so that I could go meet Victoire. Today I would see not only Victoire, but also her mother. I was a little beside myself, wondering what to expect. Truthfully, I was afraid. The rain was a stall. Still, I waited for a break.

The phone rang and startled me. I startled a second time at finding Victoire on the other end.

"You haven't changed your mind, have you?" she asked, playfully. She was accusing me of chickening out and I paused before answering. "Darling," she said. "Will I see you?"

"I'll be there. I've been sitting here waiting for the rain to let up."

"Let up?"

"For the rain to stop."

"The rain will not stop," she said. *"C'est Paris."*

"Aye," I agreed.

"My mother has changed our plan."

"Oh?"

"She would like to shop and so we can meet you at Le Bon Marché, the restaurant there."

"That's very easy for me," I said. "What time? I will have to leave to be at the gallery around two."

"Will one o'clock be good for you? We will meet you at the restaurant on the second floor."

"I will be there."

I hung up. What was I thinking? I was about to go meet with my mistress's mother. It occurred to me that I was no doubt older than the woman or at least her age. How would she regard me? I would not lie about my family, the fact that I was married with two children. And yet I was planning to be there. Such a situation called for a good stiff drink and yet I did not want one. In fact, I realized that since being with Victoire I had not had a drink. This new, accidentally discovered sobriety confused me. I certainly could not have gotten myself into any more trouble had I been drunk, but here I was, sober and not wanting a drink. What was Victoire for me? A drug? Some thrill that replaced a drug? I was using this young woman. For sex certainly, but perhaps in ways that I just didn't comprehend. Of course she was also using me. I was for her some kind of fantasy or rite of passage, but I was hardly complaining. I was a forty-six-year-old living, breathing, and irrefutable proof that evolution is some slow shit.

I arrived at the restaurant a little early, my shopping having gone smoother and more quickly than I had imagined. I'd managed to find and buy for April a soft doll that seemed suitably French and a couple of figures of mythological creatures for Will, in other words, dolls for them both. Will, even at two years, balked at my calling his figures dolls. I would simultaneously instruct and tease him by pointing out that they were indeed dolls. I had also found a necklace for Linda. I had bought it for her, would give it to her, she would thank me and coo over it genuinely and then never wear it. She had a wooden box of such gifts. And also in the bag was a necklace for which I had paid less, which I would later give to Victoire. I had no doubt but that she would wear it.

I saw Victoire and her mother before they spotted me. They came off the escalator next to housewares. Victoire was wearing a cerulean coat covered with white clouds, after Magritte but missing the overcoated men in bowler hats. She was in fact a bit of sky walking into the room. Her mother was no less pretty and sadly looked considerably younger than me. Her dark hair and strong features were nothing at all like her daughter's but she carried herself in the same way, assured, with a slight but hardly detectable bounce in her step. Her mother wore a black leather trench coat and black boots. She looked prepared for the likes of me. I waved and they saw me. To my surprise both daughter and mother smiled.

I stood up to greet them. Victoire kissed my cheeks. "That's a beautiful coat," I said.

She actually twirled. "It's new. Do you like it?"

"I do," I said.

"Kevin, I'd like you to meet my mother, Sylvie."

"*Sylvie, enchanté*," I said.

"*Monsieur Pace.*" She shook my hand. She looked me in the eye. "*Ma fille m'a parlé de vous.*"

I believed I understood her. She was from Nice and I was not used to her accent. "*Aussi*," I said, meaning *likewise*. I saw her smile and I became a bit embarrassed. "*Pareillement?*"

"Like I said, your French is cute," Victoire said.

"Please, sit down," I said. I helped Victoire with her coat and she sat beside me, her mother directly opposite. The waiter came and we ordered drinks. Sylvie asked for champagne. I, like Victoire, ordered water with gas.

Sylvie asked me something in French. I looked to Victoire for help.

"My mother wants to know if you do not drink."

"*De temps en temps*," I said.

Sylvie smiled. "I am sorry that my English is not so good."

"Your English sounds better than my French," I said.

"My mother is a fan of your work," Victoire said.

"Oh, that's really nice to hear," I said. "I'm always amazed to hear that anyone pays attention to painting anymore."

Victoire translated. Sylvie nodded.

"The gallery opening is Tuesday night. You are both welcome to come, as my guests." I was talking and I understood what I was saying, but had no idea what I was doing.

"*Merci,*" from Sylvie.

"You have been shopping," Victoire observed.

"Gifts for my children." As I said this I thought about the present for Victoire and wondered if she might be considered one of my children. She seemed, sitting next to me, at once an elegant woman and a beautiful child. I looked at her mother, perhaps with sadness in my eyes. "*J'ai deux enfants. Une fille et un garçon.*"

"*Nos enfants sont nos vies,*" she said. She raised her just-delivered flute of champagne.

"*Tchin-tchin.*"

"How long will you be in France?" Sylvie asked.

"I leave next week."

Victoire told her. Sylvie sent a question through her daughter. "Will you be back?" she asked.

"I hope so," I said, which was true enough, but hardly the answer that either of them wanted to hear.

"Victoire should visit the United States," Sylvie said.

"It's true," Victoire said. "I need to do it for my studies."

"Of course you should," I said. I was a little unnerved by this talk.

"Do you think New York is a good place?" Victoire asked.

"It's a wonderful city," I said. "I think you will like it there."

"Is not too big?" Sylvie asked.

"It's a big city," I said. "I think she will be okay."

"You will come see me there?" Victoire asked.

"I will try," I said. I wanted to look Sylvie in the eye and ask her if she knew I was fucking her daughter, but I knew she knew. What I didn't know was what that meant to her. I felt like the sort of man who might wear a smoking jacket. The fact that I never had must have shown.

"My daughter is in control of her life," Sylvie said. Her line seemed rehearsed, but no less sincere.

I nodded.

"You are too American," she said.

Whether it was meant as an insult I just didn't know, but it stung nonetheless. As with most true accusations, I saw no reason to be defensive. "I suppose that is true," I said.

Sylvie spoke in French. "My mother wants to know if all the paintings in the show are recent."

"*Oui.*"

The waiter came and we ordered food.

"I understand that Victoire's father does not know about me," I said.

Victoire did not need to translate this for her mother. Sylvie answered, "He is not an art lover."

I found this response intriguing, confusing, and terrifying. I looked to Victoire for help, but there was none there.

I became bolder. "It's okay with you that I am sleeping with your daughter?" I could tell that Sylvie did not quite comprehend, yet Victoire did not offer a translation.

"*Aimes-tu ma fille?*" Sylvie asked.

I understood her question. I looked at Victoire and then back at her mother. "*Oui, beaucoup.*" I surprised myself. I surprised Victoire.

House

Will was twelve, in the seventh grade. The snow had started on Monday late afternoon and fallen in earnest throughout the night. Even though the blanket of snow was considerable we sent the children off to school anyway. We did this because, being the sheep we were, we did not receive instructions from the school to do otherwise. Linda braved the treacherous road only to return and tell me that she thought she'd made a mistake.

"Why didn't they cancel?" I said. "It's going to be a real mess later."

"At least the plows are running," she said. "Maybe it will let up."

"Maybe. I'll be out in the shed."

"How's it coming?" she asked.

"It's coming."

"Will I ever get to see this thing?"

To this I had no answer. Actually, I did have an answer, but it was not one I could say out loud. "When it's done," I lied.

"I've heard that before," she said, perhaps playfully.

I put on my jacket and walked out through the snow. It was possible that it was not falling as hard. I locked myself inside and put on water for tea while I paced in front of the painting. I checked my supplies and noted that I needed linseed oil and rags. I always needed rags. I turned on the radio and learned that the snow was supposed to continue through the next day.

At around noon there was a banging on my door. It was of course Linda. I stepped outside and closed the door.

She looked at the door, up into the falling snow, and then settled on my eyes. "Really?"

"What is it?"

"I promise I won't peek," she said, annoyed.

"What is it?"

"The school called."

"I'll go pick them up," I said.

"I never should have taken them in the first place." She was always talking about what shouldn't have been done. She would say it five or six more times before the day was over.

"Never mind that," I said. "They're there and that's what we have to deal with. I'll get my keys."

"The weatherman on the radio say it's going to snow through tomorrow," Linda said.

"I heard. Should I take some snacks for them?"

"I'll put something together. I never should have taken them."

The plows had been busy, but so had nature and they worked together to make icy and bone-shaking roads that only became smooth at intersections and on hills. It took me considerably longer than usual to make the trip. When I did arrive I was one of many parents in a queue of cars waiting to be spotted by offspring.

April trotted, shoulders hunched, through the snow and climbed in the front seat next to me.

"Get in here and warm up," I said.

"It's so cold," she said. She stomped on the floor.

I looked at the building, at the doors. "Where's your brother?"

"How should I know?"

"I assumed you were both standing in there looking out for me. You might not talk to him, but you know what he looks like."

"I haven't seen him."

We sat there for a while, maybe ten minutes that felt like thirty. Cars came and left, became fewer.

April sighed. No one could sigh like April.

"Jesus," I said, an uncharacteristic interjection for me. "Wait here."

"Like I can go someplace."

I left the car running and walked into the school. I looked around the front hall. I saw Will's Latin teacher, a wispy woman with smoker's cough. I asked her if she had seen Will.

"Not today," she said. "I have him in the afternoon."

"He didn't come out to the car," I said.

"Maybe he's in the library," she said.

I followed her. Her coughing made me want to cough. The library was dark and empty. I thanked her and went to the main office. The tall secretary who I thought had never liked me stood behind the counter.

"I'm trying to find Will," I told her.

"Did you try the library?"

"Yes."

She called over the PA system. "Will Pace to the main office. Will Pace to the main office."

We waited a couple of minutes.

"Maybe he caught a ride with someone else," she said.

"And why would he do that?" I said, rather curtly. I put my hand to my pocket and realized that I had left my mobile phone on the kitchen table. "May I use your phone?"

"Of course."

I came through the gate and around to the phone. As I was calling Linda, the principal came out of her office.

"What's going on?" she asked.

"Can't locate Will Pace," the tall woman said. "Not in the library."

"Evelyn, go check the gym," the principal said to the tall woman.

Linda answered.

"Has Will called?" I asked.

"No. Why?"

"We can't find him."

"What do you mean you can't find him?"

"I mean I'm here looking and I cannot find Will."

"Where is he?" Linda asked.

"I don't know. I left my phone at home, so I'm in the office. Is there anyone he might have hitched a ride with?"

"I don't know. I'll make some calls. April's with you, though."

"She's in the car." That sounded bad as I said it. "The car's running and the heat is on. Make those calls. I'll look some more."

I hung up and looked at the principal. "Is there anyplace else he might be here?" I asked.

Evelyn came back. "Not in the gym."

"Let's look around," the principal said.

We walked the campus with no luck. I asked if it was time to consider a call to the police.

"That seems premature," she said. "I'm sure he's fine. Probably caught a ride with a friend."

I walked back out to the car. The snow was falling harder, hard enough that I had to sweep flakes from the windshield. I fell in behind the wheel.

"Where's Will?" April asked.

"I don't know."

"Oh, god," she said. "Where is he?"

"Can you think of anyone he might have decided to catch a ride with?"

April shook her head. She was frightened.

I blew out a breath. "Okay. He's not in the school and if he is, they'll call your mother. If he caught a ride with a friend, then he'll get home before us. So, we'll drive home and keep our eyes open. Will you help me do that?"

She said nothing.

"April, can you watch out for people walking?"

She nodded.

"Okay, let's go. You look on the right side and I'll look left."

"All right."

We slowly drove the route back home. There were surprisingly many people walking on either side of the road. April took her job seriously. She reminded me that Will was wearing a red jacket. Neither of us could recall whether he had worn a hat or cap that morning. April was clearly distraught.

"He must have ridden home with someone," she said. "That's what he did. Idiot."

I turned the defroster on full to keep the windows clear.

"I'm sure he's fine," I said.

About halfway home April leaned forward. "Is that him?"

I crunched over to the icy shoulder and honked the horn. It was Will. He walked over and climbed into the backseat.

"What the fuck," April said.

I looked at him. His hair was wet. He had not worn anything on his head. "Are you all right?" I asked.

"I think so. I'm freezing." I could see the fear in his face. He looked down at his feet.

"What is it?" I asked. I leaned over the seat to see that he was wearing sneakers. His feet were soaked.

"My feet are numb," he said.

"April, get in the back. Will, get up here."

"My feet hurt," he said.

"Get up here," I said again. "Now!"

April opened her door and got out to move to the back. I helped Will climb between the seats into the front. I turned the heat on full and directed it through the floor vents. "Take off your shoes and socks."

"What?"

"Take off your shoes and socks, stupid!" April screamed at him. She was angry and afraid.

"It's okay, April," I said.

Will got his feet exposed and under the blowing heat as I pulled back into traffic. "What were you thinking?" I asked.

"He wasn't," April said. "He wasn't thinking. A person needs a brain to think. He doesn't have a brain."

"I'm sorry," Will said. "This is making my feet hurt worse."

"That's just the feeling coming back," I said.

"I bet you've got frostbite," April said.

I said nothing.

"Stupid," April muttered, falling back into her seat. "You're going to lose your toes."

"What?" Will looked at me.

"You're not going to lose your toes."

"They hurt," he said.

"Stupid!" April shouted into his ear.

"Enough of that," I said to her.

"Dad," Will said.

"Try to relax," I said to Will, but it was meant for both of them. I wanted to ask him what he had been thinking, but I was more concerned with his toes at that moment. "Hang in there. We'll get you home and warmed up."

Linda must have been looking out the window the whole time because she was outside as soon as we drove up. She saw him in the front seat.

April got out.

"Stay here," I said to Will. "I'll get some boots so you can get inside."

"Where was he?" Linda asked as I ran past her.

"Walking," I said. "I need to get him some boots."

"The idiot was walking through the snow in sneakers," April said, heading for the house.

When I came back with a pair of my boots, Will was near tears, but not crying. I got the boots on him and helped him into the house. Linda turned off the car and followed us in.

"What were you thinking?" Linda asked.

I put Will in the chair in front of the fire in the kitchen. Linda peeled his jacket off of him. The color in his feet looked encouraging. "You scared us, honey," Linda said.

"I'm sorry," Will said.

"It's okay, buddy," I said.

"I just thought I could walk home."

"In sneakers?" Linda asked.

I looked at Will and then at Linda. "I think we can talk about that later," I said. "I'll make you some hot chocolate."

But first I had to pee. I walked down the hall to the washroom.

From outside April's door I could hear her crying. I opened her door and saw her lying facedown on her bed. I sat beside her.

"He's so stupid," she said.

"He's okay now, honey," I said.

"He's going to lose his toes."

"He's not going to lose his toes," I assured her. "Everything is okay."

She sat up and hugged me.

1979

Down at the dock the fishermen had set out. I watched their boat sputter, smoke, and churn and I wished I were with them instead of where I was. Richard took my plate back into the cantina. When he came back out he was followed by the Bummer and Carlos.

"Seems we have a new passenger," Richard said to me. Richard tossed me a bottle of water.

It was clear he didn't like it and neither did I, but it was the Bummer's show. "Want me to drive?" I asked.

"No, I'm good," Richard said.

The Bummer didn't look at me, but Carlos did. He smiled, said, "I don't take up much room."

I ignored him, watched the two of them fall into the backseat. Richard drove us back onto the road.

The Bummer was alert, almost on edge again. He checked his pistol. "Another hour," he said.

"I heard it's hot out here," Carlos said. I understood that he was not talking about the weather.

"Who did you hear it from?" I asked.

"From people who know," he said.

Richard looked over at me. "Be cool," he whispered.

I nodded.

"*Ja*, be cool," Carlos said in his annoying accent.

The road began to climb up and away from the lake when the Bummer instructed Richard to turn right onto an even less developed track. Soon the Caddy was bottoming out every few feet.

"Stop the fucking car," the Bummer said. "This is as far as this piece of shit will take us. Everybody out."

We got out and stood in the open heat. The landscape was dry and menacing. There was a sudden stiff wind and then nothing. The lake was perhaps half a mile away. I looked around for any sign of people, structures, paths, anything. There was nothing to see.

"This way," the Bummer said, heading off down toward the water.

"You don't carry a gun?" Richard asked Carlos.

"Nobody wants to shoot me," Carlos said. "Besides, guns are heavy. And they smell of oil. And you have to keep them clean."

"So, the answer is no," Richard said.

I was behind the two of them, bringing up the rear. We were passing through a wooded area. I could see a clearing ahead and possibly a shack.

"Is that where we're going?" I called forward to the Bummer.

He didn't answer. At the edge of the clearing he had us stop. We came up to stand with him. "The Nicaraguans," he said. "They use that shed. There are two more beyond it."

"How do you know this?" I asked.

Still, he ignored me. "Your brother is around here," he said to Richard. "There's a chalet over the rise."

"Tad is there?"

"He's somewhere around here."

I stared ahead at the shack. Just beyond it I could make out the wall of a white tent. Its front flap moved with the breeze off the lake. I looked left to the water and for the first time the beauty of it came to me. There was movement on its surface and some life. I felt ungenerous for not having seen it as beautiful until then. And even then I wondered if my finding it so was not some self-preservative reflex, an attempt to close out the immediate world in which I found myself. I attended to the color of the water and could not name it. It was not green, I thought, and so I knew that there was green in it, but still blue, as green as a blue can get and still be blue. We only ever spontaneously deny the presence of things that are actually there or should be there. The palms swayed.

"What now?" Richard asked.

The Bummer sat on the ground and put his back against a tree. "We wait for a while. Watch."

I looked at the sky. It was going to rain just like it had rained every day we had been there. It appeared it might rain earlier. I realized that I never spotted the clouds rolling in, only that it was raining.

Around noon it still had not rained, but I continued to feel it coming. A man walked by the shack and then another. They were not carrying rifles and that made me feel a little less tense, but hardly relaxed.

"Is that your brother?" the Bummer asked.

Richard stood and looked. "It is!" Before the Bummer could stop him he ran out into the clearing. "Tad!" he shouted.

Tad turned. Even from that fifty or so meters I could see the confusion on Tad's face. I could also see that he was in no trouble at all. He looked back to be sure he was seeing correctly. I ran after Richard and saw another wave of confusion as he spotted me and this time fear washed over him.

Tad ran to meet us. "What the fuck are you doing here?"

"We came to find you," Richard said. "We thought you were in trouble. Mom is worried sick."

"You need to get the fuck out of here," he said. "Fuck. Fuck. You really have to go. Now."

"We thought you might be hurt or in jail."

"I'm fine. What the fuck, Ricky." Then he saw the Bummer and Carlos slowly walking toward us. "Who the fuck are they?" He saw the Bummer's rifle. "He's got a gun? Jesus, Ricky, tell the guy to hide that thing." He looked back at the shed.

"What are you doing here?" Richard asked.

"Let's get back into the trees. Come on." Tad tried to turn Richard and me around.

"Are you all right?" Richard asked.

"I'm fine. But you have to get out of here. How the fuck did you find me? Fuck, Ricky."

"We're here to take you home."

"I'll be home soon enough."

"Just like that, we're supposed to turn around and leave you here." Richard was angry. "We flew all the way down here and find out you're what . . . what is this . . . some kind of drug operation?"

"Get the fuck out of here."

"Hey!" someone shouted from the shack.

"Shit," Tad said. He turned back to the voice. "Everything's all right! *Todo está bien!*"

"Who is that?!" The man had pulled a pistol from his pocket. He stopped and called back, *"Los hombres con armas!"*

The Bummer raised his rifle and leveled it at the man.

I fell down while trying to back away from him. Tad was more afraid than any of us because he knew who the other men were.

The man from the shack shouted again, *"Ven rápido!"* A man came out of the tent with a rifle.

"Fuck," Tad said. "Just run."

Carlos was already running. I ran after him. Richard and Tad were behind me. I heard a shot and turned to see the Bummer squeeze off a round. Then he was running too. We ran into the trees and kept running.

Tad kept swearing and saying we were all dead, fucked. "I can't believe you showed up here. You're a fucking English major."

Fear pushed me into anger and I grabbed Tad by the front of his shirt. "Listen, you fuckup, your brother came down here for you."

He slapped my hands away. "Get the fuck out of my face."

The Bummer pushed Tad. "Keep moving."

"Who the hell are you?" Tad asked. He leaned as if to fight. "Touch me again, asshole."

The Bummer pushed the barrel of the rifle into Tad's side. "I said, run, motherfucker."

We all ran again. I felt a pop in the back of my calf, the leg of the sprained ankle. It hurt like hell, but I kept running. We ran past the path we had taken to get there and it ended at the lake. We stopped behind a sandy berm and a stand of short palm trees. The rain started to fall. It was sudden and hard. Carlos inexplicably tried to light a cigarette, but failed.

Tad was too confused and mad to say anything.

"What now?" I asked the Bummer.

"We wait and then get back to the car."

It rained for about fifteen minutes and then stopped as suddenly as it had started. I was soaked. I looked over at Richard. A bullet hit the palm tree right next to me. Stupidly, I turned to look instead of ducking down. I saw two men with rifles hunched and running toward us. The Bummer shot at them and the men fell to take cover. Richard was shaking. I suppose I was also, but I didn't feel it. The Bummer pushed his pistol toward me.

"What?" I asked.

"Take this," he said.

I ducked my head into my shoulders as a bullet hit just above me.

I reached out and grabbed the gun by the grip. "What am I supposed to do with this?"

He looked me in the eye and said, "Shoot everybody but me!"

"What did he say?" Richard asked me.

I turned to Richard. "He's crazy," I said. More shots rang out. "Fuck."

"Bummer!" Richard called. "What now?"

I turned back to the Bummer. His face was flat in the sand.

"What is it?" Richard asked.

"Bummer," I said. "Bummer." I moved closer to him. "I think he got shot," I said to Richard.

Carlos crawled over. He turned the Bummer over. The was a neat hole in his forehead just about his left eye.

"Oh, shit!" Richard screamed. His legs started running even though he was lying on the ground.

I glanced up and over the mound and saw the men running away. They were not looking back for us at all.

"Is he dead?" I asked Carlos.

"Oh yeah," he said.

"They're gone," Tad said. "But they'll probably come back. In fact I know they'll be back."

"The car is this way," I said. I put the Bummer's pistol in my pants.

Richard was badly shaken. "What the fuck were you doing?" he asked his brother. He pushed him in the chest.

"I was doing business with them until you showed up."

"Fuck, fuck, fuck," Richard said.

"He's dead?" Richard asked Carlos again.

Carlos wasn't paying any attention to Richard. He was looking up the hill, looking for danger.

"Come on, let's go," I said. I wanted to get home. I needed to get home. That was all I was thinking. I kicked Richard's leg. "Let's go."

Carlos grabbed his shoulder bag.

"Asshole, aren't you going to take his damn picture?" I asked, staring Carlos in the eye.

"Why? Nobody's going to miss him."

Paris

I was unsure what I felt as I left that lunch with Victoire and her beautiful mother. I dropped the gifts I'd bought for my family at the hotel and kept the necklace for Victoire with me. There was a very light drizzle and I decided to forgo the metro and walk up the rue du Cherche-Midi to Saint-Germain and the gallery. I imagined what any number of my friends would have said if they had witnessed my lunch, Richard especially. They would have told me that my affair was at the very least ill-considered, and if anything the mother should be the object of my desire. As I walked, as I listened to those imagined voices, I fell more deeply for Victoire and felt increasingly more stupid with every degree of descent. Yet I had not been so relaxed in years.

I arrived at the gallery, chatted with Etienne about the placement of the two remaining paintings, and then followed my same route back to my hotel, entertaining the very same thoughts and arriving at the same concluding feeling. I climbed the stairs to my room and was about to shower when the phone rang.

It was Linda.

"I was going to call you," I said.

"Well, the snow has stopped."

"Glad to hear it. How are you? The kids?"

"Everyone is fine," she said. She sounded distant. "Why don't you tell me what you're doing?"

I was thrown by the question and its directness.

"I know what you've been doing," she said.

I didn't know what to say, so I said nothing.

"You've been getting drunk again and I don't like it."

"What?"

"You expect me to believe the clerk rang the wrong room. You were out drinking with Etienne or you were passed out drunk."

I decided to attempt a skip over this. "I was just with Etienne discussing the placement of the remaining pieces, but I haven't been out drinking with him. The opening is tonight."

"I don't know why you have to be there for this," she said.

"I think it's really helped for me to be involved," I lied. "Especially tonight. You know how people like to see the artist. Is anything wrong?" It was a stupid question as she had already expressed her concern about my drinking.

She was silent on the other end, the stupidity of my question having not gotten by her.

"Linda?"

"How much have you been drinking? When I called the other night, did you not answer because you were drunk?"

"I didn't answer because the phone did not ring," I told her. Another lie.

"How much are you drinking?"

"You'll be happy to know that I have not been drinking at all." I realized how ludicrous that sounded.

"Kevin."

"Okay, I've had wine with dinner. That's it. Call Etienne and ask him if he's seen me take a drink. Call the clerk and ask him if I've been stumbling in."

Her silence betrayed her disbelief. I felt accused and oddly relieved. She was not concerned that I was having an affair, but that I was drinking too much. I wondered if I was just so much a bore that she could not imagine me having an affair, then came back with the sad truth that she actually trusted me. I was being accused and should have been, but was guilty of something else, something worse. My pathetic history, my sorry past failure had surfaced as effective camouflage for my current indiscretion.

"Really," I said. "I feel good."

"Will really misses you," she said.

"I miss him, too. I miss all of you. Just a few more days and I'll be home."

"I'm about to do the shopping. Do you want anything in particular from the market?"

"That yogurt I like," I told her.

"That's all?"

"Plenty of fruit."

"Okay. Be safe," she said.

"I love you," I said.

Linda hung up.

Etienne was hopped up on coke before the evening had even gotten started. I had seen him like this before and it was hardly alarming, but mildly annoying for the fact that many already answered questions were repeated a few times. He told me three times that the Spanish couple from Marseille who had bought a large canvas of mine would be there that night. Each time I responded with a tonally unchanged, "That sounds promising."

I was standing alone on the back patio looking up at the now clear sky. Nothing obstructed the bright fingernail of moon. I was drinking cranberry juice, wishing that Linda could see me.

"Is that cranberry juice?"

I turned around to find Richard.

"What the hell are you doing here?"

"Nice greeting," he said.

"Sorry," I said. "You surprised the hell out of me." I gave him a hug. His coat was cold.

"I was in London at the BM for some work and I thought I'd pop over for the big event."

"That's great," I said, but I knew I was hardly convincing.

Richard looked around the patio and through the windows back into the gallery. "They told me you were back here. What I saw inside looks good. Very elegant. *Très* French."

"Thanks."

"To the French," he said, raising his glass of red wine.

"*Tchin-tchin.*"

"So, how's it going?" Richard asked.

"Good. I'm looking forward to getting home. How long in London?"

"Just a few days."

"So, you talked to Linda," I said.

"No, why?"

"You've never been a good liar."

"Everything okay?" he asked.

I held up my glass.

"Cranberry juice?"

"Believe it or not, I haven't had a drink in a week. Haven't wanted one."

"That's a good thing," he said.

"Aye."

I could see through the windows that more people were showing up. Etienne would be coming soon to drag me into the mix.

"I'm glad you came," I said to Richard.

"*Bonjour,*" this from Sylvie. She had come onto the patio without my noticing. She gave me the customary two-cheek kiss.

Richard was immediately taken. I could see it on his face.

"Sylvie, I would like you to meet my friend Richard."

Richard shook her hand. "*Enchanté,*" he said.

I was saddened to see Sylvie's flirtatious smile. She turned to me. "*Victoire sera bientôt là.*"

I glanced to find Richard staring at me.

"So, you are also a friend of this wonderful artist," he said to Sylvie.

I could see Sylvie struggling to understand what Richard had said when Victoire came out to join us. Her cerulean cloud coat was draped over her arm. She came and stood next to her mother, smiled, and nodded hello to Richard. The distance between the two of us was awkward and telling.

"*Ma fille, Victoire,*" Sylvie said. Richard shook her hand.

"*Bonsoir, Victoire,*" I said.

"*Bonsoir, Kevin.*"

Richard was staring at me again.

"*Maman,*" she said. "*Voyons les peintures.*"

The women excused themselves and left us on the patio.

"You dog," Richard said. "You're not going to say that this isn't what it looks like."

"No, I'm afraid it's exactly what it looks like. A goddamn train wreck."

"The daughter? How old is she? Twenty-five?"

"Twenty-two."

"What about the mother?" he asked.

"What about the mother?"

"She's beautiful, in case you hadn't noticed. And she knows?"

"Yes."

Richard whistled. "To the French," he toasted.

"I'm an idiot," I said.

"Well, I don't know."

"Take my word," I said.

Before I was forced to offer any details, Etienne came out to fetch me. "You must be on the floor," he said. "People want you."

Richard raised his glass again as I walked away.

House

Linda and I had children late in life. We married fairly young; I was twenty-six and she was twenty-five. However, it took her nearly twelve years to convince me that we should try to have a child and then several more until we actually conceived April. She persuaded me by telling me I was being selfish by refusing. Fact was I liked the idea but didn't think I deserved to be a father, didn't imagine I would be any good at it. It's possible that I wasn't any good at it after all, though I thought I was fairly decent at parenting when the kids were younger.

We left the city just after Linda became pregnant with April. I took a job at the Rhode Island School of Design because I thought I needed to be a more responsible, parent-type person. We moved into the house built by an artist friend, what not-so-affectionately became called the house from hell. Would that it had been haunted. At least that would have been interesting. To say that it was designed and built by an artist was to underscore the fact that it had not been designed and built by an architect or, say, someone who actually knew how to build a house. It was completely, absolutely, almost admirably energy inefficient. We could see a quarter-inch of daylight through every join of every window and door. Part of the house, ostensibly a studio, was unheated altogether, yet connected to the rest of the house by a wide, doorless descending stairway corridor and so robbed what heat there was from the living area. The sewage system was designed to recirculate the smell of, well, sewage, through the house and around the yard. Linda hated the house. I hated that Linda hated the house. We bonded over hating the house. The most insulting detail of the house's history was that it had been created, endorsed, and financed as an art installation. My friend had owned the land and had talked a nearby museum of contemporary art into sponsoring his project. He built a bad house with a few interesting angles and then after the exhibition bought the house from the museum for a fraction of what a house in the area might have cost. I didn't mind that he had gotten paid to build his house and that he had gotten a great deal to own his house, but every day I was offended by the fact that some serious and decent young artists might have been supported by that money. It became a living metaphor for what was wrong with the art world and art business.

We nearly went broke trying to heat the place, but what it did offer was a painful yet effective object lesson on what we did and did not want in a house. After April was born we moved into a big block of a New England farmhouse. Squares of rooms set into one big square with rectangles plopped down on a big square of land. It was functional and well crafted. It was simple and right. The new house ordered my life, ordered my work, and I felt good. But after some years the squares began to feel square. The block of a house felt like a block. And my world began to have too many corners and not enough space.

Our summers on the Vineyard saw us in the same saltbox house every year and though the cove behind opened to the horizon, the house there merely echoed the house at home. Corners everywhere. I felt cornered. My work became predictable like the angles of my spaces. The paintings were purchased, and I found that to be merely injury layered onto insult. Then, when April was seven years old and Will three, I sealed up the small barn and began the painting. Even the first stroke was completely private, wholly my own.

The painting began after my return from Paris. Linda was pleased to have me home, but still angry that I had been away. The show in France had been a success, so that made my absence a little more tolerable. But whatever palliation the sales offered, my newfound retreat into my newly fortified studio undid.

I mentioned that first stroke. I made that mark of that large canvas and it was alone there for several weeks before I touched the work again. It was not large, that single mark. It was not symbolic or metaphorical. It was not even perfect. It was my first mark. It would be covered and never seen again, but it would be there, always the first mark. Like a first kiss, it could never be repeated.

Richard never balked at my locking him out of the studio. He regarded me with a cocked head like the RCA dog's, but let it go by making fun of me. "Oh, the mad scientist at work in there," he said. We were sitting in the coffee shop in the village.

"Pretty much."

"Galatea?"

"Very funny."

"So that's completely over?" he asked.

"Doesn't it have to be?"

Richard shrugged.

"Yes, it's over."

"Would you do it again?"

I looked across the room at a couple of young women having their frothy coffee drinks. "No," I said. "Knowing what I know now. No."

"What do you know now?" he asked.

"I have no idea."

Richard nodded.

I raised my teacup in a toast.

"I was afraid you'd actually fallen in love," he said.

"I did fall in love," I said. "I admit that. It felt wonderful. At the time it even felt right."

That fact found me on occasion and depressed me. As did that large canvas depress me, though it perhaps served to round out my corners, my angles; it also reminded me of my indiscretion and my love and that depression led me, several years later, to drink again. Not a lot, but what isn't a lot? Not a lot is what we drunks say. Any was too much. Any was noticeable and was noticed.

I was not so much susceptible to guilt, but shame was a different story. Will was eleven. We were on the Vineyard and a storm had come up suddenly. We were in Edgartown doing some shopping when it became clear that we needed to get home. The four of us were in the car and I was about to turn the key when Will said, "Dad, should you be driving?" Shame. I stopped again.

1979

Somewhere, somehow, I had lost my watch. I looked at my wrist and it was not there, only the light outline of where it always was. I looked around through the sand. The watch held no sentimental value, was not at all expensive or special in any way, but I wanted to know the time. I wanted to know the precise time. Not for any practical or strategic reason, but only because I didn't know anything precisely or distinctly at that moment. I asked the others for the time and none of them had it. I could not believe that among the four of us there was not one fucking watch. I seethed about this while marching, limping, rather, while ostensibly leading the way back to the car.

"Your leg okay?" Richard asked me.

"It'll have to be. The Bummer is dead. This is fucked up."

I stopped and said as much to the sky as to the others, "I need to know what fucking time it is?!" I looked at Carlos.

Carlos checked the sky. "Two or three," he said. "Thereabouts."

"I don't want two or three," I said. "I want two forty-seven. I want three-oh-six. I don't want thereabouts."

"You're not in the States," Carlos said. "This is El Salvador. All they have here is thereabouts."

Richard looked up the hill and then to me. "Are you all right? Want to rest for a while?"

I glared at him.

"Stupid question," he said.

"I don't know exactly where we are," I said. "The car is up there somewhere. I don't know who is or isn't chasing us." I looked at Tad. "I thought I might be able to know what the time is, exactly, precisely, certainly."

"Can we discuss this later?" Tad said.

"You know, this is all your fucking fault." I pointed a finger at him.

"Nobody asked you to come down here," Tad said.

"Your brother asked me to come down here," I said. "Fuck you, Tad. You really are just a fuckup."

Tad looked at Richard.

"We really need to keep moving," Carlos said.

"You shut up," I said. "Carlos, my ass. Have some guts and use your real fucking name. Hans? Heinz? Himmler?"

"Come on, Kev, let's go." Richard looked scared.

"All right," I said. "Let's go sort of, kind of this way, more or less."

We wandered for another couple of hours and though it appeared we had a lot of daylight left I was becoming convinced that we would not find the car. I did think that if we just kept walking up that way we would perhaps find the road.

"What's that?" Tad said.

There was a glint west of us and down the hill. It was the Cadillac. I had never been so happy to see an oversized American gas guzzler in my life. That awkward joy quickly evaporated and was replaced by a sense of dread. That dread was reasonable enough.

We stood next to the car, looking around, resting.

"The Bummer is fucking dead," Richard said as if it was news.

I said nothing. There was nothing to say about that.

I wanted to tell Carlos to stay behind, but, even though I thought I could follow the roads back to the city, I considered that we might need him. One wrong turn would be all it took.

Richard fell in behind the wheel and I into the seat next to him. When he turned the key, nothing happened. He tried again. Not even a click.

"Fuck me," Tad said.

"Turn the key again," I said to Richard. I lowered my window. "It's not the battery."

"Then what is it?" Richard asked. "You know anything about cars?" This to Carlos.

"Nothing."

Tad got out. "Pop the hood."

"What are you doing?" Richard asked, getting out. "You don't know anything about cars."

We were all out now.

"Staring at it never works," Richard said.

"You came down this bumpy-ass road in this?" Tad asked. He wriggled himself far enough under the car to reach the starter motor. I could just see him through the spaces in the engine.

"Dad's car did this once," Tad said.

"Did what?" Richard asked.

"Try it now." He pulled himself out by grabbing the bumper.

Richard reached in and turned the key. The engine turned over, started. "What did you do?"

"You knocked the starter motor coming down this road."

"Let's go," I said.

I regarded our momentary glee at the starting of that engine and marveled at the idiocy of the human spirit. Our world was fucked. Someone with us had just been shot to death, our hatred of him notwithstanding. Homicidal Nicaraguan drug dealers were probably right behind us. And we were brightened because a Cadillac's 472-cubic-inch engine had started.

Richard drove us slowly, carefully up the trail. He stared through the windshield and frequently asked my advice about avoiding big rocks and deep ruts. Tad scanned all around us like a frightened poodle.

It was dusk when we came to the road.

Paris

I would not suggest that spotting me with Richard unnerved Victoire in any way, but she respected my physical space and practiced admirable and much-appreciated discretion. I watched her as she prepared to leave with her mother and found, to my pleasant surprise, that I just couldn't let her go like that. After all, Richard had deduced the obvious truth. I walked up behind her and helped her with her coat.

"Will I see you later, my love?" she asked while her face was turned away from me.

"It's late," I said. "I'll spend some time with Richard. I'll see you early tomorrow, if that's okay."

"Of course," she said.

Sylvie kissed my cheeks good-bye.

Then, Victoire, and as she kissed my second cheek, she whispered, *"Je t'aime,"* so softly that even her mother did not hear. I barely heard it, but could not have missed it.

They left and I returned to Richard.

"So, do you have time for me tonight?" he asked.

"I suppose."

Etienne was very pleased with the evening and also crashing. He told me that we would talk about the business later. I chatted with a few more people and was finally able to break away. I was reminded by listening to myself that my charm, what charm there was, lay in my utter lack of charm. Richard stood away and appeared amused by my rehearsed, genuine, and comfortable awkwardness.

"It's a strange thing," I said as we walked across the river toward the first arrondissement. "If one is awkward consistently for long enough the awkwardness becomes safe harbor. Is that somehow disingenuous or deceitful?"

"I think the term is *Janus-faced*," he said.

"Thanks."

"Victoire," he said to the moon. "She's a beauty."

"There are lots of beauties out there," I said.

"Right. Aren't you above it all."

"Yes, she's beautiful," I agreed. I stopped at the middle of the bridge and looked down at the Seine.

"Don't do it," Richard said.

"Don't think I haven't thought of it." I looked at him. "So, my friend, am I crazy?"

"No, but you're a carrier."

"Am I?"

"Yep."

"This can't lead to anything," I said.

"Nope."

"I've got a beautiful family."

"Yep."

"Is this pretty much how this discussion's going to go?"

"Yep."

"I actually have feelings for this woman."

"I'm sure you do," Richard said. "I don't even know her and I have feelings for her. And for her mother." He laughed softly. "Don't listen to me. I know you've done the math, but here it is again. She's nearly twenty-five years younger than you. When she's thirty-five, you will be fifty-nine. Not quite old, but you see where this is going. Your daughter will be nineteen and will hate your guts. Your son will be fifteen and he'll excuse himself from the dinner table so he can go to his room and jack off to internet images of Catherine Deneuve."

"I preferred the monosyllabic routine."

"I call a spade a spade."

"Careful."

"So, what now?" he asked.

"Good question. I suppose I have to break a sweet young woman's heart." I had an urge to drop something, anything, into the water below, but I had nothing.

"Come on, let's go have a drink," Richard said, slapping me on the back.

"No, I need food. I haven't had anything since I didn't eat lunch."

He looked at me.

"What?" I said.

"Really. No drink?"

I shook my head.

"She must have some pussy."

I caught myself before I could become angered by his remark. Instead, in my head I heard Victoire's whispered *"Je t'aime"* and saw her green watercolor. "You have no idea," I said.

"Tell me, does she make you feel younger? Is that part of this?"

On the face of it this was a reasonable enough question. I thought about it. "No," I said. "In fact, I feel older. I would have to, wouldn't I? But the thing is, I don't care. She doesn't care. She really doesn't. So, I don't care."

"How moving."

"It's all I've got."

House

Linda was a little surprised that I was not returning to my studio to continue working after dinner. She asked if I wanted to watch a movie and I said if she wanted to, which was as good as a no. I did however switch on the television news while she was performing her evening stretches.

"Are you okay?" she asked.

"Look at the weatherman," I said. "Is there really anyone that color? He's orange."

"Tanning bed," she said. "You're watching the news? You never follow the news."

"Hey, I know what's going on."

She laughed. She bent over at her waist, grabbed her ankles, and appeared to try to kiss her knees.

"We need to talk about something," I said.

She came back up. "Sounds serious."

"It is."

Will burst into our room. "It's April," he said. "Something's wrong."

We hurried downstairs after him to find April sitting on the toilet. She was leaning over, in obvious pain and distress.

Linda knelt beside her, "Honey?"

"She's sick," Will said. "I heard her crying."

"Are you cramping?" Linda asked.

I could see blood on her fingers and on her thighs. I pulled Will away and closed the door most of the way. "You go on to your room," I told him. "Everything's under control."

Linda came to the door and looked at me. "She's burning up."

"Should we give her some Tylenol?"

"Mommy," April said. She only used that word when she was afraid.

"I'm right here, baby."

"There's so much blood," April said.

"I see, honey," Linda said. "Take deep breaths."

April cried out softly. I could just hear her.

Linda came back to the door. "There's so much blood," she said. "Something's wrong. I think we need to take her to the emergency room."

"No," April said.

I pushed open the door and looked at her face. "I think that might be a good idea," I said.

"Did you tell her?" April asked me.

"Tell me what?"

I looked at April. I had the fleeting thought that her letting the secret out was orchestrated, but as quickly decided that couldn't be.

"I was trying to tell you just now," I said.

"You promised," April said.

Linda was staring at me, her hand flat on top of April's hair.

"You were going to break your promise."

Linda looked back down at April.

"I'm pregnant." April didn't look up, but down at the bit of bloody toilet paper in her hand.

"You're what?"

"Pregnant," April repeated.

Linda shot me a deadly look and then looked all around, assessing. She pushed April forward and peered into the toilet, let her back down. "You're having a miscarriage."

"I'll take her to the hospital," I said.

It was as if I was not there at that moment. Linda stroked the child's hair. "It's going to be okay."

April cried.

Linda looked again at me and I understood that I was to leave the room. I closed the door. Will was in the hallway, scared to death.

"Is April all right?" he asked.

"She's okay, son," I told him. "Go into your room and watch a movie or something."

"But she's okay, right?"

"Yes. Woman stuff. Okay?"

Will walked off and into his room.

Linda came out of the bathroom. Frankly, she scared me by the way she was looking at me. "You knew about this?" she asked.

I nodded. "I was trying to tell you when Will walked in."

"How long have you known?"

I hesitated, then whispered, "April made me promise not to tell."

"I'm her mother!"

"Yes, right. I wanted to tell you, but she was so insistent."

"Did you take her to the doctor?"

"No, she said she had it under control."

"Those were her words?"

I felt cold inside. "I don't remember her words, but that's what I understood. She only told me because I said it would remain a secret. I didn't know what was going on until she told me. I'm sorry. She was opening up and I was so worried about betraying her."

"You're an idiot."

"I was respecting my daughter's privacy."

"I am her mother," Linda said, forming each word distinctly. "I'm supposed to know about these things."

I looked at the closed bathroom door and moved away to the bottom of the stairs.

"She didn't want you to know."

"What if she had said she wanted to kill herself? Would you have told me that? I've got to go back in there."

"Is she all right?" I asked.

"I can't believe you. What, did you get off on the fact that she was confiding in you instead of me?"

I had never even thought of that, but in hearing it I did recognize that I had gotten some good feeling from being secretive, complicit with her. It also occurred to me that Linda was angry because she had not been the chosen confidant. But I said, "I'm sorry. I never thought of it like that. I just wanted her to be comfortable."

"Is she comfortable now?"

"Are you suggesting that I'm the cause of what's happening now?"

She ignored my question.

"Is she all right?"

"She'll be fine."

Linda went back into the bathroom and closed the door.

I glanced into Will's room and saw that he was sitting on the edge of his bed, playing a video game. I then went to the kitchen and put on water for tea. I sat at the table and waited. I wasn't certain for what I was waiting, but I was waiting. Waiting seemed like the correct, the right, the prudent thing to do. I heard Linda move April back to her room and I regarded just how quickly the locus of safety had shifted, just how quickly April had allowed her mother to assume her role as mother. Just as quickly Linda had closed me out. And rightly, I imagined, as I obviously did not know how to help. Still, I felt that my part in all of this had been engineered. But that was okay. As long as my little girl was safe, it was okay. It didn't matter whether she hated me for betraying her secret. She was okay. It didn't matter that I now had to face Linda's rightly shaped anger. April was okay.

Linda came into the kitchen and sat at the table opposite me. If she had been a smoker she would have been lighting one. She looked at my tea.

"I made a pot," I said.

She looked at my face and then out the window. She wasn't shaking her head, but she was.

"I'm sorry," I said, again. "How is she?"

"She's still cramping."

"Does she need to go to the emergency room? Do you want me to pick up anything at the pharmacy?"

She shook her head. She yawned. She often yawned when she was nervous, confused, or angry. And now she was all three. "I'm taking her to my doctor in the morning."

"That's a good idea," I said.

"I'm glad you approve," she said. She laughed mockingly. "You wouldn't know a good idea if it slapped you in the face."

I knew right then what it was like to be slapped in the face. "Linda, I know I fucked up. I really was just about to tell you when Will came into our room. She made me promise."

"So, what? She made you promise."

"I wasn't trying to keep it from you."

"How is Will?"

"He's shaken up, I think. He was playing a game and I didn't disturb him. Does she still have a fever?"

"Ninety-nine point three. Not high."

"Still a fever."

"I gave her some ibuprofen."

"Are you going to forgive me?"

Linda didn't answer that question, didn't look again at me. She got up and left me at the table.

I looked across the dining room at a small canvas of mine. There was no blue in it. It was often pointed out that I avoided blue. It was true. I was uncomfortable with the color. I could never control it. It was nearly always a source of warmth in the underpainting, but it was never on the surface, never more than an idea on any work. Regardless that blue was so likable, a color that so many loved or liked—no one hated blue—I could not use it. The color of trust, loyalty, a subject for philosophical discourse, the name of a musical form, blue was not mine. And by extension green was not mine. In fact, in Japanese and Korean, blue and green have the same name. As blue as the sky is, the color came late to humans.

The reds, browns, and ochers that I used so much were the colors of the cave dwellers, but they had no blue on their walls. I sometimes hated blue. I could not stand to see the Prussian blue in the waves of Hokusai. For that reason, for my disdain of the color, I knew it was important, that my dislike of it was a function of fear and that fear, like all fear, was a function of lack of ken. I looked at the shadows in the room, shadows full of blues. Cobalt, cerulean, ultramarine, emerald green, Guillet green. Van Gogh wrote to his brother Theo about the intensity of cobalt. He was crazy, you see.

1979

Richard drove with me leaning into the windshield or out the window on the lookout for potential holes where we might bottom out. It was slow going, but it seemed preferable to proceeding in a hurry and breaking down altogether. For the first time Tad and Carlos got to look at each other in the backseat.

"Who the fuck are you?" Tad asked.

"I'm nobody," Carlos said. "Same as you."

"Who is this guy?" he asked his brother and me.

"Like he said." I looked back at them both.

"Where are we going?" Tad asked.

"The airport," I said.

Richard looked over at me.

"What?" I asked.

"I'm afraid my passport is at the hotel. Sorry."

I studied the rough lane in front of us.

"I didn't want to lose it," Richard said.

I touched my back pocket and felt my passport still there. He was right of course.

I'd lost my watch of all things, right off my wrist, and hadn't noticed. I glanced back at Tad. "Do you have your passport?"

"Yeah, I have it."

"We just drive into town, grab your passport, and drive to the airport. We'll look less suspicious if we have our bags anyway."

"We're in so much shit," Tad said.

"What are you talking about?" Richard asked.

"They're going to catch us."

"Shut up," I said.

"We go back into the city and we're fucked," Carlos said. "There's a damn revolution going on if you hadn't noticed. And I'll wager the whole place is on fire by now."

I turned my attention back to the road. "It's getting hard to see."

"How far until we're on the next road?" Richard asked.

"I don't know," I said. "We're going so slowly. I just don't know. It looks completely different coming back." I turned to Carlos. "Do you know just where we are?"

"Not really. Everything looks the same out here to me."

"Stop the car," I said to Richard.

"What?"

"Stop the car."

He did.

"Get out," I said to Carlos.

He stared back at me.

"If you don't know anything, then you're of no help. We don't need you. Get out."

"Fuck you," he said.

I pointed the .45 that the Bummer had handed to me at him. "Get out of the fucking car."

"Okay, maybe I do know where were are. Roughly."

"Hell, I know *roughly*," I said.

"Just another couple of miles and you'll be back on the road to San Salvador. Then I can get you to town. I know a lot of the soldiers. So, can I ride with you?" He relaxed and fell back into the seat.

I faced the front.

"Sorry about the passport," Richard said.

"It is what it is."

"I need to piss," Tad said.

Richard gave me an exasperated look and stopped the car. We all got out and relieved ourselves. The just-fallen night was dead still and quiet. Fog was forming in patches down on the surface of the lake, but above us the sky was clear. I looked at the brush into which I was peeing and wondered just what else could go wrong. I had not yet seen a snake and imagined that one might show up now and bite me on my penis. Everything was so absurd. I recalled the punch line from a joke: "You are going to die, Kemosabe."

I took over the wheel and we moved on. Since I couldn't see the dangerous holes very well, I drove faster than I should have. In about an hour we made a left onto the smoother but not much more developed road. It was a relief.

We drove on and veered onto a still better road. There was no traffic at all until I spotted a couple of taillights ahead of us. They were not moving.

"Stop," Carlos said. "Turn off your lights."

I did both as quickly as he said it.

"What is that?" Richard asked. "A checkpoint? Well, we don't have anything to worry about."

I could hear Tad behind me, muttering, "Fuck, fuck, fuck."

"Turn around," Carlos said.

"Are you crazy?" Tad said.

I looked back at Carlos.

He looked me in the eye in a way he hadn't before. "We go back about a half mile. There's a dirt road that goes around this. It's not bad. Goes through a tiny village that's not even on the map."

"What do you think?" I asked Richard.

"Go around it," Tad said.

Richard nodded.

I drove back and turned up a steep road that seemed to lead in the completely wrong direction and then it curved back. Things then became really confusing as the road started switching back down a mountain road in the pitch darkness.

"Do you know where we're going?" I asked Carlos.

"Yes, it's a twisty road, but it comes around back to the highway."

The road became very narrow. I couldn't see clearly but I knew there was a steep drop off the right side. That was when we met headlights.

"What the hell?" Richard said.

"What is that?" from Tad.

"I think that's a bus," I said.

"Shit," Richard said. "Can we get by him?"

"I don't think so."

The driver of the bus was out and walking toward us. I started to get out of the car. "Carlos, let's go." I needed his Spanish.

The driver was a short, wide man, built like a refrigerator. We met him in the mix of our headlights. He pointed at the Caddy and spoke rapidly.

"He says you have to get out of the way," Carlos said.

"Ask him how I'm supposed to do that."

Carlos did.

The driver became more animated, pointed at his bus and then at our car. He spoke again.

"He wants us to back up."

"Why doesn't *he* back up?" I wasn't trying to fight with the man, but I was afraid to try backing up.

"He says he cannot back up the bus, that you can see better backing up a car. You have to back up."

"What if I don't?"

A couple of people stepped out of the bus and fell in behind the driver. Two young men. They looked frightened. The driver turned and said something to them. Then they yelled at me, looking no less frightened, but now threatening.

"They say we have to back up," Carlos said, as if I needed a translation at this point.

"All right, all right, tell them I'll do it."

We returned to the Cadillac and got in.

"We have to back up," I said.

"Fuck that," Tad said.

"Don't have any choice. He might decide to just push us off the road if we don't do it."

I looked behind us and saw only darkness. The bus rolled to us and the driver honked his horn. I put the Caddy in reverse, but the backup lights didn't improve my view at all.

"Look out on that side for me," I said to Richard.

He leaned out his window. "Shit! It goes straight down."

I tried to hug the side of the mountain on my left, so much so that I scraped the side of the car, tore off the driver's side mirror. The noise was alarming. It became clear that the bus was not going to pass on the outside, so I drifted back to the right. Back some thirty yards we found a wide place. Carlos and Richard kept yelling at me that I was right on the edge.

"Then move to the left of the goddamn car," I shouted. "Put all the weight over here."

The bus climbed the wall of the mountain a little to get by us. Its light raked the side of the Cadillac and then it was a dark rattle beside us, actually brushing us once. Tad let out a short squeal. I leaned against my door, trying to will the car to stay where it was. Then it was over. The bus was only taillights behind us.

"I think we're okay," Richard said.

I drove forward a few yards to move the car to the middle of the road. I put my forehead to the steering wheel.

"You okay?" Richard asked.

"No, I'm not fucking okay. Are you okay?"

"Can we just get out of here?" Tad said.

We rolled on.

Paris

After dinner, after his drinks and his astonishment over my having only club soda, after a brief description of my meeting Victoire but by no measure detailed, I put a somewhat tipsy Richard into a taxi and sent him off to his hotel in the fourth. I wanted the long walk alone back to my hotel. I followed the river on the right bank and crossed over on Pont Neuf. I'd put myself well away from my hotel and half-knowing ended up nearer to Victoire's flat. It was well after eleven and yet I continued on Saint-Germain toward her. A light rain fell. I pulled up my collar and marched uphill on rue Monge. Finally, I was standing on the street outside Victoire's building. Her windows were dark. I didn't know if her mother was staying with her. I didn't know if the boyfriend she mentioned early on was with her. A lamp switched on inside and I hoped that she might come to the window and look out, not that she would be able to recognize me in the shadows. Against not only my better judgment, but any judgment whatsoever, I climbed the four flights of stairs and stood outside her door. I listened, heard nothing, then tapped lightly. Victoire opened the door a crack, smiled, and let me in. Her smile did so much for me.

"I knew you would come," she said. She closed the door and hugged me. She was naked under her robe.

"I guess I needed to see you," I said.

She looked over at her closed bedroom door. "Of course you needed to see me. My mother is using my bed. I'm pleased you're here."

"I should go," I said. "I needed to see you and now I've seen you."

"No, stay."

"I don't want to wake your mother. This was a bad idea. I actually thought she might not be here."

"Don't worry," she said.

I pulled her close and kissed her. I turned my face and looked at the bedroom door.

She put her hands on my cheeks and directed my face at her again. "She is a heavy sleeper."

"I was a little worried that your boyfriend would be here."

"And yet here you are. Have I charmed you so?"

"Are you absolutely sure your mother won't wake?" I sounded like a pathetic teenager.

"I'm positive. And about my boyfriend, he broke up with me. Just like I predicted."

"Why would he do that?" I asked.

"Because I told him that I am in love with you."

"You did," I said. "Why would you tell him something like that?"

She bit my lower lip and let it go. "I told him a thing like that because it is true. Why else would I tell him a thing like that?"

I kissed her softly. "You might tell him to make him jealous. To make him want you more."

"I don't care if he's jealous and I don't want him to want me more."

I walked backward and brought her to the daybed under the window, the very place we had first made love.

"I really am afraid of disturbing your mother," I said, again.

"I will be quiet," she said and dropped her robe.

I tried to kiss her, but she was looking down, unbuckling my belt and opening my trousers. She reached in and wrapped her cool fingers around my penis. She said something, but I missed it, I didn't understand her. She pushed down my pants and shoved me into sitting on the bed. She knelt down and put me in her mouth. After a very short time I pulled her up to my face, kissed her mouth. She looked at me, smiling, confused.

"What is wrong?" she asked.

"I want your face near mine," I said.

"D'accord."

"I want your voice next to my ear."

"*D'accord.*"

"I want your breath in my mouth."

"*D'accord.*"

We lay on the daybed, her head on my chest. We looked out the window at the sky, but could see nothing.

"That was beautiful," I said.

"Do you have a better secret to tell me?"

I felt the perfect weight of her head on me. I touched her hair. I knew I would tell her my secret. I had never told the secret to Linda and I didn't know why, except that I believed that there had to be some secrets that remained secrets. I had come to love the power of secrets and saw every painting as a secret waiting to be revealed. Or not. "I do," I said.

"Okay." She snuggled into me like a child awaiting a bedtime story. "Okay, I'm ready."

"When I was your age I went to El Salvador. How I ended up there doesn't matter. It was a bad time, just before the civil war."

I could feel Victoire's silence.

"There were a lot of people shooting, though I didn't see a lot of that. But I did come upon a child who had been killed. She was so small. It was like she wasn't real. I didn't know what I was seeing."

She squeezed my shoulder.

I described the scene and told her about the father and the boy and about digging the grave and the secret that had been shared by only me and the boy I called in my head Luis.

"That is terrible," she said.

"It still haunts me."

"Of course it does."

I said nothing.

"Kevin? What's wrong?"

"That's not the secret."

House

I considered myself a significant and singular failure as both a husband and a father. Sitting alone in the dead-quiet kitchen I heard clearly what I should have said to April when she first insisted that I keep her secret. I was supposed to have said, "I'm sorry, but that is not a secret I can keep." Simple. "You can hate me if you need to or want to, but this is something your mother has to know." Obvious. I was left to scrutinize my actual motivation for so glaring a misstep. How could I have missed something so apparent, plain to see? There was no reason I could come up with that was at all flattering. Perhaps I was not strong enough to confront a child. Perhaps I was somehow pleased to have been the chosen confidant and jealously protecting my office. Or perhaps, and more likely, I was just too much of a numbskull to see the simple, obvious, conspicuously correct course of action. The sad truth was that I was guilty of all three, a kind of potpourri of moral depravity.

Will came into the kitchen and sat with me at the table.

"It's late," I said.

"Couldn't sleep."

"That's because you're still dressed. Have you been playing that game this whole time?"

"Pretty much."

"What's the object of the game?" I asked.

"You know, kill all the demons before they kill you, then kill them again, get killed, start over."

"Like life," I said.

"Is April all right?" Will asked.

"She's fine." I looked at his face. He looked so much like his mother. "You're a good brother, Will. Your sister got pregnant."

He had figured out that much, I could see that. "What happened?"

"She had a miscarriage," I told him. "I guess her body wasn't ready for her to be pregnant."

"So, she's not pregnant anymore." He said it as if it was a case of problem solved. "She's okay, right?"

I nodded. "She will be. She's going to be feeling a lot of different things. You have to go easy on her."

"Okay."

"Want some tea?"

"I don't like tea."

"Scotch?"

He laughed. "Why is Mom mad at you?"

"Well, I knew about your sister and didn't tell her. Your sister insisted that I keep it to myself and I did."

"You should have told Mom," he said.

"Yes, you're right."

"Are you okay?" he asked.

I looked at his face. My son was so kind. I liked him so much. "I am okay, Will. Thank you for asking me that."

"Well, I guess I should go to bed," he said.

"Take your clothes off first."

He smiled. "I'll do that."

It was either in the yard, the kitchen, or the car, but Linda asked me a question so disturbing that where it was asked was unimportant. She asked, "If you could keep something like this from me, what other secrets are you hiding?"

Let's say it was in the car, because there is no escaping a conversation made in an automobile. "I have no secrets," I lied.

"No?" She laughed. "You've got one the size of a building in our yard."

There was nothing I could say to that.

"I never asked you about Paris," she said.

"That was ten years ago."

"What was ten years ago?"

"Paris," I said. "What are you talking about?"

"Why did you have to be there?"

"That was ten years ago."

She looked out the passenger side window. She hardly spoke to me after that. There were no accusations, there was no screaming, there was nothing, not even sighing. She yawned. The kids noticed the distance between their mother and me, but didn't address it. How could they have? I thought that my, in my mind, ancient, infidelity had finally come home to roost. Metaphors are like oil paints: when you work wet they can get away from you.

I toyed with the idea of confessing the affair with Victoire then appreciated that to do so would not be to build trust, but to make me feel better about myself. As much as I needed to feel better about myself, I could not hurt Linda any more than I had. And then that thinking began to sound like mere rationalization. I was beginning to face an annoying truth that I had long avoided. I was unhappy. I looked at my life and it was clear that I should by all measures be happy, but I was not. And it was not that way because I had isolated myself in my work. I had used my work as a refuge, a sanctum, a hiding place. However, this harborage turned out to have but one way in and one out and I had lost sight of it. It could have been argued that ten years earlier I had succumbed to a banal midlife crisis, but now I was falling victim to something far worse, a late-life revelation.

"Linda is not speaking to me," I told Richard. We were sitting at our usual table in our usual coffee shop. "And of course neither is April."

"Is April mad because you broke your promise?"

"No, she's mad because I didn't break my promise. She thinks that if I truly loved her I would have told her mother."

Richard shook his head.

"Don't shake your head. She's right." I played with the little packets of sugar and fake sugar. "She's absolutely right."

"How's Will?"

"He's okay. He's still talking to me, but I suspect he too blames me for all that's wrong. But he's a kind soul. He's nice to his old man."

"He's a good kid."

"Yes, he is."

"Where is all of this leading?" he asked.

"What did you tell Linda about Paris?" I asked.

"I told her that you weren't drinking."

"That's it?"

"That's it. Why?"

"She brought up Paris the other day. She's not stupid. I suspect she guessed what was going on."

"That was ten years ago. Tell me, do you ever think about her? What was her name?"

"Victoire."

"I remember her mother."

"I think about her often," I said. "She told me as I was leaving that I was breaking her heart, but I think I actually broke my own."

"Wait, are you saying you still want to be with her? You're not thinking that you can go find her."

"No, I'm not that crazy. That's not even a ship that could have sailed. I am apparently stupid, but I'm not crazy."

"No, but you're a carrier."

"That's what you told me ten years ago."

"It's still true."

I asked the passing waiter for more coffee. "I don't know if Linda will ever forgive me. I might have fucked everything up completely. What was it you used to call Tad? Fup? Well, that's me."

"I never told Linda anything."

"I know," I said.

1979

I was still shaking a little when the taillights of the bus were out of sight. It didn't help matters that it started to rain.

"Let's go," Tad said.

"It's not far back to the main road," Carlos said.

The road made one more wide curve and then headed down a steep grade that was becoming increasingly slippery with the rain. The wipers were on high and I could barely see ten feet. Then, as if a tap had been turned, the rain stopped. The road became even steeper and we actually slid to a stop at the intersection with the highway. Now on the other side of the checkpoint, I turned right and sped toward town. I felt sick as we passed by the airport and had half a mind to get out and wait for them there, but then it was only half a mind. Once I saw the airport, once I knew where we were, I pulled the car off onto the shoulder.

"Okay, Carlos, this is where you get out," I said.

"What the fuck?" he said.

I kept seeing the photographs of dead faces and I imagined the poor, wretched people who paid money to this monster to take a look. "And you can leave your notebook."

"Fuck you," he said, his accent more obvious.

I pointed the muzzle of the Bummer's pistol at him. Richard jumped, threw himself against the passenger door. Tad sank away too, but, uncharacteristically, he said nothing.

"What are you doing?" Richard asked.

"Richard, open the door and pull the seat forward so that Carlos can get out."

"Put that thing away," Richard said.

"Listen to your friend," Carlos said.

"The notebook stays here. The camera too. But you, you're getting out of this fucking car."

"You won't shoot me."

I was out of my head and I knew it and that made me appear calm, I think. "I will shoot you. Tell me, who will miss you? I'll shoot you, take your fucking picture, and drop it off at the Dutch embassy."

He looked at my eyes. He didn't know me and that was a good thing. He didn't realize, however, that there was no way in the world I could pull that trigger. He didn't call my bluff.

"Fuck you," he said again. He got out and looked at the highway forward and behind. I imagined that he was trying to find some way to draw soldiers' attention to us, but there were none.

I drove away quickly. Richard was staring at me, shaking. "What the hell was that?"

My hands were not steady on the wheel.

"Were you going to shoot him?" Richard asked.

"Hell, no."

"You looked like you were going to shoot him."

"Maybe, I don't know."

"Are you all right?" he asked.

"So, now you're a badass," Tad said from the backseat.

I ignored him. "I'm all right," I said to Richard.

"What is this book?" Tad asked. I could hear him open the notebook.

"I just hate that guy." It seemed this place was full of people to hate. "The idea of him charging those people to look at those pictures."

Richard sighed in agreement. Then, "Kevin, what the fuck. What if that gun had gone off?"

"What is this?" Tad asked again. It was dark back there and he couldn't see much of anything.

"They're dead people," I said.

"What?"

I looked at Richard. "Let's just get your passport and get out of this fucking country."

Some seven or eight blocks from the city center we found ourselves in some trouble. Groups of men and women, mostly young men, trotted and ran in all directions. We saw no soldiers, which was at once a relief and a concern. A concern because I had no idea what that meant. The car rattled like it might fall apart and the engine was now misfiring worse than ever. Without discussion we had long abandoned the notion of returning the vehicle to Crackerjack. I felt bad for the man who had rented it to us, but honestly I didn't believe he cared about the car now; there was too much else going on in his world to concern himself with a Cadillac Coupe de Ville. I parked on a fairly quiet street just about half a mile from the hotel.

"I'm afraid that if we drive any deeper into downtown we might not be able to drive out," I said.

Richard looked at the activity in the streets. "You're probably right." He looked off in the direction of the hotel and then back at me. "You should stay here with the car. We need it."

"I don't know," I said.

"I'll stay here with the car," Tad said.

"That's not happening," Richard said. "You come with me."

Tad looked at me and I stared back. "Fuck both of you," Tad said.

"If we're not back in an hour, go on to the airport," Richard said.

"I'll be here when you get back. One hour, six hours. I'll be here. Now go, hurry up."

I watched as they trotted away.

"Don't run!" I called.

They had been gone fifteen minutes and I began to wonder just how long I would wait there for them. I felt conspicuous sitting in the car like a cop on stakeout or standing beside it like a badly dressed pimp. The notebook was still in the backseat. I had managed to get it away from Carlos but now didn't know what to do with it. Burning it occurred to me as a good idea. The album was heavier than I remembered. So much death. I hadn't known how dense death was. Just yards from me the contents of a garbage can were in flames. I took the book to the can. It started to rain lightly. I opened the ring binder and pulled out one of the stiff plastic pages and tossed it in. The edges curled and the fronts of the Polaroids turned white, bubbled, and disappeared, the faces dissolved, melted. The heat from the can was intense even with the rain, which fell harder. The Bummer's pistol was under my shirttail in the front of my jeans. I didn't know anything about guns and was afraid the heat might set it off. I in fact had a notion to toss it into the can. I put the book under my arm and was attempting to move the pistol to the back of my pants when there was a gunshot and something struck the can. I think I let out a short, high-pitched scream. The notebook fell, I fumbled with the pistol, turned around. The pistol was in my hand. I saw the soldier as I turned, perhaps twenty feet away, a small man with a rifle, the barrel pointed at me. He fired at me again, I can still see the flash, and the pistol in my hand went off. I must have pulled the trigger though I did not feel the action and I have no physical memory of it. It was extremely loud, the report. My ears rang and the world seemed to slow down. The man fell backward. My mouth and throat went immediately dry. I threw the gun into the street where it slid under a truck and I looked all around. I remember that I didn't know where to put my feet and so I did a little jig. A couple of people at the cross street pointed at me and ran away. I stepped forward to see that there was no way the man could be alive. I could not have described his face. The pistol had sent a bullet into his right cheek and through his head. The pistol did it, not me, I told myself. His dark blood spilled out through his hair and onto the already wet sidewalk. I would have thrown up if I had had anything in me. I leaned over the man. I couldn't tell whether he was young or old. "Hey," I said. "Hey, man, get up," I said. Of course he didn't. He was wearing light-blue socks. The acrid smell of a brewery found me. I looked to see the big tanks across the intersection. I walked away only to turn around and walk back. I looked at the dead man again. He looked like a drawing by Käthe Kollwitz. In the darkness, he was a charcoal likeness of a human being. I finally knelt down beside him and put my finger to his neck, clumsily looking for a pulse and I found none. I rubbed my hands together as if I was cold and still I do not know why I did it; I was not cold at all. I remember the action all too well, rubbing my hands like a stupid fly. I stood up to see that my knee had dipped into the man's blood. Again I peered up and down the street. I could see people passing by at the intersection, but no one was near me. I could not remain there, but where could I go and know that Richard would find me? I realized that I would get back into the car and drive to Richard.

I fell in behind the wheel. The Caddy balked when I tried to start it, but started after a third try. I looked in the rearview mirror and saw the man's feet, hoped that they would move. They didn't.

I pulled slowly away, as if that made me harder to see. I had killed that man and with him a part of me evaporated. I could feel myself leaving, and yet staying behind on that sidewalk, lying down on that sidewalk beside that small man. I was burning in that can's fire. Maybe the small man had a wife, children. He would not be coming home to them. I had taken him away from them. For a brief second I tried to justify my action, however accidental, by reminding myself that he had shot at me and that just made me hate myself more.

Paris

"If I had not been in that country I could not have shot that man, I would not have killed him," I said.

Victoire cried beside me without sound. Her mother was apparently still asleep in the bedroom. If she had come out then I would have been completely lost and probably unrecoverable. I had told Victoire something I had never been able to tell Linda or had chosen not to tell her. For twenty years I had not shared this with Linda. But here I was, telling this young woman with whom I had absolutely no future. Perhaps that's why I could tell her.

"I'd better go," I said.

"Why?"

"Well, your mother is liable to wake up any minute now. I'm sorry I put all of that on you. You're so young and beautiful and you didn't need to hear that. It's ugly and I'm sorry."

"I asked you for a secret." She held me. "My secret is that I tried to killed myself."

I have to admit that for some reason that news did not surprise me.

"I'm okay now. I was depressed. But I'm okay now."

"I'm afraid that I am hurting you. That I will hurt you," I said.

"Of course you will," she said. "I know you cannot be away from your children. I don't have some fairy-tale dream that you will come live with me. I am young but I am not naive."

I nodded. "No, you are anything but naive," I told her. Again she had left me feeling like the younger one. I touched her cheek. "You are such a lovely person. You are pure color."

"*Lovely*, that is an interesting word."

"Isn't it," I said.

She took my hand.

"So what is this, us, what we have?" I asked.

"Love," she said.

"*Love*," I repeated as if listening to the word. "That's such a big word."

"Just love me," she said.

"I do love you," I said.

House

April's coolness was hardest to take. Though I had been on the verge, the very rim of betraying her trust, I had not in fact done so, as I had been interrupted by nature. What was more was that my crime, in her eyes, her complicity notwithstanding, was that I had somehow shown a lack of care and love for her by not breaking her confidence, by actually keeping her secret to myself. I was in what might have been called a lose-lose situation.

I believed that Linda would eventually forgive me or at lease excuse my behavior, but she would never forget and so things would always be different. What was significant was that I did not want her to forgive me. It was not only that I could not forgive myself, that was a given, but somehow I needed some kind of change and that change had to come as a conciliation with my past. I didn't know what such a rapprochement would look like, but I had to explore the possibility of it.

The secret that I held closest, the secret that I never told anyone, that I shared with no one, was that I had married Linda without loving her. I wanted to love her. I liked her immensely, thought the world of her, respected her, but I could not then say that I loved her. I probably came to love her. I certainly shared life with her enthusiastically, happily, willingly. I was pleased that she was the mother of my children, but my heart never ached for her, my skin never longed for her touch. I had in fact used her. I had used her to feel whole again, normal, to feel like a good man after what I had done in El Salvador. She held my head and stroked my temples when I was depressed without knowing the cause. She considered me the moody artist. And that I was. The irony, of course, one of them, was that my depression actually fed my work, made my art better, gave it a gravity, a depth that it hadn't had before. A certain amount of guilt came with that truth, a guilt that never went completely away, a guilt that became easier to live with and yet more profound.

Again, Linda and I were older parents because it took me so long to accept myself as worthy of that step. Mainly, however, I agreed to it because she wanted it so much. I might have done it because I finally wanted it as well, but I don't honestly know if that's true.

We were camping by a lake in upstate New York. Linda was tired from the hike and I had just set up our tent. It was cool but not cold in May. She sat on a log on the shore and looked west across the water.

"What are you thinking about?" I asked as I sat beside her. The sun was just beginning its decline. "It's going to be a nice sunset."

"Yes, I think so," she said.

I picked up a stone and skipped it.

"I can never do that," she said.

"Here's a question for you," I said. "You find the perfect skipping stone." I picked up a flat rock. "Say this is it. Imagine that this stone is beautifully flat, that it's Payne's gray in color, just like this one, oval but not egg-shaped. It's made for the art of skipping."

"Okay," she said.

"It's perfect. Do you throw it or keep it?"

"You throw it," she said.

"Really?"

"Yes." She took the stone from me. "You can keep it until you die and then you'll never see what it can do."

"What if you mess up the toss?" I asked. "It just goes splash into the water. No skip, not even one."

"How is that different from dying with it in your pocket?"

I looked at the water.

"You don't agree?" she said.

"No, I agree completely."

"So, what's the point of all this?"

"About this baby thing."

A light rain began to fall, but we didn't move. I might not have loved Linda, but I belonged with her.

1979

That small man, that small, charcoal likeness of a man who lay dead on that street would not be going home or anywhere for that matter. I didn't really care about justice. I didn't care about honor, probity, or character. I thought only about getting back to my own home, my safe home, my safe bed. I drove the route I thought Richard and Tad would have walked. I turned onto a street with a disturbing amount of pedestrian traffic. People walked in the middle of the street, caring nothing about the rain or the car I was driving. I leaned on the steering wheel to see as I inched forward, tried to find Richard and Tad in the crowd. Young men peered in through the windows at me, angry men, and I was tempted to roll up the windows in spite of the heat. Their eyes were threatening, but no one acted against me.

The light was unreal, which is to say it was all too real, harsh, coarse, shrill. I would not have been surprised to see mobs carrying torches, chanting. I imagined that in some part of the city people were doing just that. People walked across the street in front of the car and behind me. A woman slapped the Caddy's hood with both hands when I inched toward her and got too close. The man with her glared and shook a fist, shouted something.

I saw Richard and Tad. In fact they saw me first and were trotting toward the Caddy. They weaved through the crowd and squeezed into the car. Richard tossed my bag and his into the backseat.

"I thought you were going to wait," Richard said.

"I had to move on. Did you get it?"

He showed me his passport.

"What a fucking mess," Tad said from the back.

"It sure is," I said. "This is what I was afraid of." I needed to be headed in the opposite direction, but the intersection ahead was crammed with bodies. I had to turn around where I was. "I don't know how to turn this whale around."

There was loud noise, a boom or crash, a cannon or a car wreck, somewhere we couldn't see. People at the intersection ran in all directions, some toward us. I pushed the nose of the car slowly left into the crowd.

"What are you doing?" Richard asked.

"I'm trying to turn around!" I tried to back up. People pounded on the trunk and the hood, bouncing the car on its weakened shocks. I moved forward again, sounded the horn. Doing that made a couple of men even angrier. I ignored them and that made them angrier still and the anger it seemed was contagious. The men and others took to punching and kicking the Cadillac, rocking us. A man reached in and grabbed me by the front of my shirt. I raised the window.

"I don't like this," Richard said. "I don't like this one little bit. Get us the fuck out of here."

"I'm trying."

"They're going to turn us over," Tad said.

I got the car pointed in the right direction and I pushed through. There was another loud boom behind us and that sent our attackers running, shouting, and screaming again. I didn't even bother to look into the rearview mirror, just concentrated on moving the car forward.

"It's a fucking tank," Tad said. "I saw it. It just went through the intersection. A fucking tank!"

There was an opening in the crowd and I covered a little more street. Finally I was able to speed forward, if fifteen miles per hour could be considered speeding. The gap in the throng opened even more and once we were away from the center we were on our way to the airport.

Richard stared at me. "What do you think?"

"What the fuck do you mean *what do I think*? I think we're fucked.

I think we'll never make it to the airport. I think a tank is going to
blow us up!"

He turned back to the window.

We did make it to the airport and it was surprisingly, eerily calm.
We parked and abandoned the Cadillac for good in a lot for cargo
pickup. We went to the ticket counter and Richard bought three
tickets to Los Angeles, the next plane out, and paid for them with
his Master Charge. It all went so well, so smoothly that I was unnerved. It was late and the airport was all but empty. Our flight
would leave seven hours later at seven thirty. That was plenty of
time for everything to turn bad, I knew that. The soldiers still pa-
trolled the terminal with the same nonchalance they had when we
arrived, and just like then they gave us long looks. It was as if nothing was happening in the city. The ticket counters went dark and
food vendors had already shut down their carts.

"I'm starving," Richard said as we walked away from the counter.

"Me too," Tad said.

"I suppose that's a good thing," I said.

They looked at me.

"It means we're still alive, so to speak. What would it mean if
we weren't hungry?"

Richard cocked his head. "Since when did you become a bright-
side person?" he asked.

I was looking back at Richard, but all I could see was the face of
the small soldier, his light-blue socks.

"What's wrong? We're in the airport. We're about to go home."

We sat in chairs across from the baggage claim area. I reached
down and rubbed at the pain in my calf.

"Kevin?" Richard said.

"I'm okay."

"Did something happen?"

I looked at Tad sitting just on the other side of Richard, then
around at the deserted airport. A man operated an electric floor

cleaning machine not far away. The machine appeared to get away from him every few feet and he'd have to regain control. The noise of the machine was strangely soothing. "Did something happen?" I repeated the question. "The last three days happened."

"We'll be back in the States soon," Richard said.

"Not soon enough." I shook my head to clear it. I looked again at Tad.

Tad caught me looking at him. "What?"

"Tad, are you holding?"

"What?"

"Are you holding?" I asked. I looked at Richard, then back at Tad. "I don't want to get back home just to get locked up because that idiot has drugs on him."

"Who are you calling an idiot?" Tad said.

"Do you have any drugs on you?" Richard asked, sounding the words exaggeratedly slow.

"No," Tad said. "As a matter of fact." He looked at both of us in turn. "If I had anything I'd be doing it right now."

That was reasoning I couldn't argue with.

Tad kicked out his legs and crossed his ankles, put his head back and closed his eyes. "Now, just leave me the fuck alone."

"We've got a long wait," Richard said. "Let's all just relax."

"Aye." I let my head rest against the wall behind me and shut my eyes too. Behind my lids I relived the killing in excruciating detail. I fought the urge to open my eyes and instead watched the event over and over, wanting desperately for it to end differently, but it never did, wouldn't.

Paris

I had walked a lot through the rain since coming to Paris. I could think of no paintings with rain in them and I realized I wasn't about to make one, either. But as I walked through the sixth arrondissement so late at night, so early in the morning, I saw the blue of rain, how it tinged the darkness of night sapphire and how Alice blue made lavender the leading edge of morning. The rain fell with no feeling for me, was as indifferent to me as I was to it. All it did was make me wet and cold.

I would be home two weeks before Christmas, a holiday that I had never fully embraced. I understood that it was not a religious celebration but a secular one, yet I still could never find the flow of it. I would go through the motions for Linda, help her string the lights I found offensive and help her find and put up a tree that I considered a sad sacrifice. The kids would also feign excitement for Linda. They were hardly wanting for anything, but still, like the little kids they were, they loved to open wrapped gifts—rather, they loved the look on Linda's face when they unwrapped gifts. So we would awake earlier than our custom, sit around uncharacteristically in our flannel pajamas and robes, and break into presents. It was always a nice time and Linda would be made happy.

I was eager to return home. Without drink I felt closer to my family in spite of the geographical distance. I would have said that I felt like some old self, but better, I felt like someone altogether different. I didn't know myself and it felt good. And at the same time, being already out of Paris in my head, I was missing young Victoire. I was in love with her the way I was never in love with Linda, but it had nothing to do with being with her. Perhaps I needed her to be just an idea.

It was four in the morning when I walked into the hotel. The clerk was not at the desk, so I sat in the lobby to wait for him even though I could have simply reached across and grabbed my key from its cubbyhole. The nattily dressed man finally came back and was just a little startled at seeing me.

"*Monsieur Pace*," he said.

"*Bonsoir, Pierre*," I said. "Or is it *bonjour* now?"

"*C'est le matin.*"

"Any calls?"

"*Non.* Not tonight."

"You probably think I'm a foolish man," I said.

He walked the key over to me. "Why do you say that?"

"You are very kind to me," I told him.

Pierre shrugged. The phone rang. I had a feeling as he walked across the room that the call was for me. I stood and walked toward the stairs. He answered the phone and turned to me and nodded.

"Just a moment. I will ring his room," he said and gestured for me to run upstairs.

I took the stairs two at a time, unlocked my door, and actually lay on my bed before the phone had a chance to ring. I feigned grogginess as I answered.

"Did I wake you?" Linda asked.

"It's okay. I had to get up anyway to answer the phone," I said and listened to her soft laugh. That relaxed me. "I wasn't sleeping well anyway."

"I'm sorry to call so early."

"Everything all right?"

"Will has a fever."

"How much of a fever?"

"One-oh-two. He looks tired and says he feels bad."

"Sore throat?"

Linda asked Will how his throat felt. "He says it burns."

"What is it, seven there?"

"Yeah. I gave him Tylenol thirty minutes ago. The fever just came on so suddenly. He came and sat on my lap and I could feel how hot he was."

"I'm going to try to change my ticket. I can probably be there in the morning."

"You don't have to," she said.

"I'll check on it, okay?"

"All right."

"Well, no school tomorrow," I said.

"That's for sure."

"Let me talk to Will."

She put Will on the phone.

"Hey, little buddy," I said.

"Hi, Dad."

"You feel pretty bad, eh?"

"Yeah."

"Try to get some sleep, okay?"

"Okay."

"Dad?"

"Yes, buddy?"

"Nothing."

"No, what?"

"Wally Reynolds got a hamster."

"He did? What's the hamster's name?"

"I don't know," he said.

"Is it cute?"

"Kinda."

"Would you like to have one?"

"No. A turtle."

"We'll talk about it when I get home, okay?"

"I miss you." His voice trailed off a bit.

"I miss you, too."

House

I felt an urge to return to El Salvador. I needed to find that lost piece of myself, whatever that meant. That was how I talked to myself, being accustomed, as I was, to making no sense. I sat in my studio and stared at the painting. I recalled the previous night. Well into the morning I could not sleep because of a pain in my left calf. I thought I had pulled a muscle, but I could not figure how or when. It ached and caused me to sleep fitfully. It was a familiar pain and then I remembered the injury from El Salvador. The pain was the same pain from thirty years earlier, but when I finally pulled myself from bed and walked to the shower, the pain was gone. All that was left was the memory of the revisiting of the pain, of the hurt. I was spooked by the ghost of the pain, its having felt so real. I studied the painting.

Plato would have me believe that my painting was an imitation of something. In fact my perceptions of the concrete things were tenebrous representations of some ideal. So I, the painter, was imitating an imitation, making a simulacrum of a simulacrum. Fuck Plato, I thought, the painting in front of me was not an imitation, not a representation, but the concrete ideal. My perception of it might well have been a representation, but the painting, well, it was the painting.

I locked up the shed and walked into the house to find Linda in the kitchen. I spoke without any throat clearing, vocal or gestural. "I know that you're angry with me. I get it. I think that you will get over it. I just want you to know that what I am going to say has nothing to do with any of this."

She looked at me and I could see that she was a little afraid.

"I'm going to take a little trip."

She sat in the chair nearest her.

211

"I am not leaving you. I would never leave you. I just have to take this trip. I need to go to El Salvador and I can't really explain why."

She didn't speak.

"I don't mean to scare you, but this is something I have to do."

She nodded almost as if she understood something.

"I always knew something happened down there," she said. "I asked Richard, but he wouldn't say anything."

I looked at her face. I had kept the secret to myself at first because I didn't want her to think of me as a bad man, because I didn't want to think of myself as a bad man. It was too scary for me to talk about it. Then, slowly, it became a secret that I kept because it belonged to me and finally I didn't know whether it was fear or selfishness that had me guarding it. You keep a secret long enough and it simply cannot be told or will not be told.

"But you won't tell me what it is," she said.

"I will tell you. But I cannot tell you now because I do not want to eclipse what is in the air regarding April. I was wrong. I was stupid. I do not resent your anger, but understand it. April's anger is more confusing to me, but it is what it is."

"Okay."

"I want to leave pretty soon."

"How long will you be gone?"

"I don't know. I'm sorry to leave you with the kids," I said.

"We'll be all right."

"I know that. You're so capable. That's one of the things I like about you." It must have occurred to her that I had not used the word *love*. I would tell her about the girl and the boy and the hand. I would tell her about the little soldier in the light-blue socks. But I would not tell her the real secret. I would not tell her that I had married her without love. As I thought about that I wondered why I was going to El Salvador at all.

1979

I think Richard and I were astonished by how easy it was for us to board the plane. Tad of course took it all in stride. Given the trouble just miles away, we were also surprised at how empty the flight was. We settled into our seats. I didn't look at Richard. I didn't look at anyone. I closed my eyes and I was asleep before we took off. I dreamed about being locked in something the doctor called a sleep cabinet and fighting the urge to dream. The doctor kept coming in and taking my temperature with a thermometer shoved up into my armpit. The doctor would laugh wildly and tell me I was lucky, then say *sweet dreams* before leaving. I could hear him though I was unable to wake, but I fought dreaming.

I awoke still buckled into my seat, thinking, rather hoping, that I had managed to sleep through the seven-hour flight, but only about forty minutes had elapsed. Richard was asleep and snoring beside me. Tad was across the aisle, staring through the window at the morning sky. I opened the shade to look out my own window, but the sun made me shut it again. Still, I was pleased to have my own window. The flight attendant came by and I asked for a beer and she smiled a smile that was not judgmental about my drinking so early. When she delivered it I thanked her for the beer and her smile.

I thumbed through a *Time* magazine that had an article about the so-called situation in El Salvador. I was saddened by the fact that I had been right there and had no idea whether what I was reading was true. But I read it all and at the end knew nothing more. I apologized to Richard as I stepped over him on my way to the toilet.

I had to wait in the aisle behind a handsome man who flirted with the handsome flight attendant. He said something that caused her to blush when she saw me. She stepped back into the galley and the man turned to face me.

"Heading home?" he asked. He studied my dirty clothes, my over-all ragged appearance.

"Yes."

"Where is that?"

"Philadelphia," I said.

"It's a mess back there," he said.

"Philadelphia?" I asked.

"No, El Salvador," he said. "What were you doing there?"

"Vacation," I said. "You?"

He gave me an incredulous look. "Journalist."

It seemed odd to me that a journalist would be leaving just when so much was happening. "Why leave now?"

"They don't pay me that well," he said. A woman came out of the washroom and we let her pass. The man didn't enter. Instead, he continued our conversation. "What kind of vacation?"

"Just a vacation." I pointed at the washroom door. "Are you going in?"

"Oh, yeah."

I sat on the arm of an empty seat in the last row and waited. In short order he was out again. "All yours," he said.

I closed and locked the door and looked over at my face in the mirror while I peed. I looked so much rougher than I had before the trip. In addition I was extremely filthy. I hadn't realized just how much dirt was on me, on my clothes, on my face, in my hair. I looked like I had been in a firefight and I understood the interest taken in me by the journalist. He was again chatting with the attendant when I came out.

"My name is Ben," he said. He reached out to shake my hand.

"Hello, Ben." I didn't offer my name, but started up toward my seat.

He followed me. "I'd like to talk to you," he said.

"I'm tired," I told him without looking back. "I'm going to get some sleep."

"Just a minute of your time," he said.

I turned to face him just a couple of rows shy of Tad and Richard. I was angry and confused and being confused made me angrier. I caught his eyes and held them. "Listen, I'm in no mood to talk to you. I'm not going to talk to you. Please don't bother me. I might do something you won't like."

The man held up his hands and backed away.

"Thank you," I said.

Richard got up to let me back into my seat. "Who's that guy?" he asked.

"Reporter." That was all I said.

Now Tad was asleep, his feet up in the empty seat next to him, his back to the window.

"So, are you going to tell me what happened while we were grabbing my passport?"

"Nothing to tell."

"Kevin."

I looked around. The seats behind us were empty. "This is between us, right?"

"Of course."

"I'm not fucking kidding around," I told him. "You can never repeat this. Do you understand?"

"Okay."

"A soldier came up to me while I was trying to burn Carlos's book."

"Yeah?"

"I didn't see him and he shot at me."

"The fuck," he said. "At you?"

"I turned around and I was holding the pistol." I stopped and looked over at sleeping Tad and behind us again. "I shot him."

Richard didn't say anything. I wasn't looking at him so I don't know if he was looking at me.

"I shot him," I repeated. "I don't know if I meant to do it, but somehow the gun went off."

"In the leg, right? You shot him in the leg," Richard said.

"He's dead," I whispered. I looked at Richard's hollow expression. "I killed him."

"You all right?" he asked.

"Well, no."

"He shot at you. What were supposed to do?"

"You can't make this any better," I said.

"It was self-defense."

"Don't talk."

"What were you supposed to do?"

"I was supposed to be in Philadelphia."

Richard stopped talking.

Paris

Victoire surprised me at my hotel the afternoon before my departure that night. I had called her to tell her of my plans to leave. My son was sick and I had get home as soon as possible.

The clerk called me. "There is a young lady here to see you," he said. "Would you like me to send her up?"

"Please."

I opened the door and waited for Victoire to step out of the elevator. I greeted her with a long hug. She kissed me and I kissed her back, but then moved away.

"I'm sorry I have to leave in such a hurry," I said.

"I understand," she said. "You are a good father."

"I don't know about that," I said. "I should be there now."

She sat on the bed and watched me pack.

"*Je t'aime*," she said.

"I know. I love you, too. I hope you know that."

"I do," she said. "I also know that I will not see you again."

I looked to see if she was crying. She was not. "I'd like to think that's not true," I said.

"We both know it is."

"I suppose."

"If I came to the U.S., would you find a way to see me?" she asked. She reached up, put her hand on my arm, and gently pulled me to sitting next to her.

"That would be difficult," I said.

"I could come live near you and you could hire me to teach French to your children."

"That wouldn't be a good idea."

"I guess not."

"I'm sorry," I said.

"When do you have to leave for the airport?"

"In a couple of hours."

"Then you have time to make love to me," she said.

"I don't think I can. I think I'm too sad."

"Then we can be naked and hold each other."

"Okay."

"Do you want me to go to the airport with you?" she asked.

"No."

House

The flight was faster and smoother than my last flights to and from San Salvador. In 1979 I had flown through Miami. This time I was routed through Dallas, with a layover long enough for me to decide against a variety of fried airport fare. I shared the plane to San Salvador with families and couples, all wholesome, on their way to a vacation destination. There might have been some business types traveling solo forward in first and business class, but back in economy I was the singular loner. The plane was wider than the one in 1979, two rows of seats three deep instead of two. The perky Pan Am stewardesses were replaced with a sturdy-looking effeminate man and an even sturdier-looking nunnish woman with a Southern accent. Their competence was a comfort, as I had no doubt that either of them could open the emergency door upside down underwater. The level of comfort was incongruous with my slowly growing fear. I was cold to my center as I realized that I would soon be landing in a country in which I was guilty of a capital crime. I entertained the notion that I was going there to be caught, that I would be required to pay for my crime. Nothing could have been less true. Still, I wasn't sure why I was going.

I sat by a window, a young couple between me and the aisle. The woman smiled at me and I smiled back.

"Are you on vacation?" she asked.

"Yes," I said.

"We're finally going on our honeymoon," she said. "*Honeymoon*, I hate that word."

"That's nice," I said. "That you're going on your honeymoon, not that you hate the word."

She must have noticed my ring. "Is your wife on the flight?"

"No."

"Is she waiting for you there?"

The husband cleared his throat, a signal that she was talking too much.

"My wife is dead," I told her.

"Oh, I'm so sorry."

I perhaps should have experienced a bit of guilt for that lie, but I didn't. The lie actually felt good. It hung in the air like a kind of thin curtain between us. The lie felt good because I had taken control of the narrative around me.

The husband put his hand on the wife's forearm, I assumed to stop her if she thought to speak again.

I looked out my window at the blue nothing. I felt freer, lighter.

"She died suddenly," I said without turning to her. "No one knows why. Just fell down dead."

"Oh my," she said. "I'm so so sorry."

I turned to her. "She looked a little like you," I said.

The woman offered a weak smile, then grabbed the SkyMall catalog.

Ilopango Airport could have been any airport. The carousels were the same, the chairs were the same, the customs agents wore the same bored faces. Except for the man facing me. My mustachioed officer gave me a long look that I wouldn't have called hard as much as strangely curious, perhaps ironic.

"What brings you to El Salvador?" he asked in perfect English.

"The climate," I said.

He nodded. "Planning to visit Lake Ilopango?"

The question caught me off guard and I realized I was paranoid. "Why, should I?"

"It's a beautiful place. But there are many beautiful places." He adjusted his desk light and studied my passport.

"I'll probably get there. I'm going to drive around, I think. I like driving in the mountains."

"You've been here before?" he asked.

"No." I was three passports into the future and I was certain he had no way of knowing I had been there before.

"*Hablas español?*"

"I understand a little. *Hablo un poco.*"

He nodded. "Phrase book?" He smiled.

"Pretty much."

"It took me a long time to learn English," he said. "It was very difficult."

"I find that hard to believe," I said.

He turned my passport over and over.

"I'm an artist," I said. I didn't know why I told him that. "A painter."

"Will you make any paintings here?"

"No, just looking."

He gave my passport one more long study, looked again at my face, and stamped the passport. "Have a nice stay."

Paris

I landed at Logan early in the morning. Whatever snow there had been was mostly slush now. Everything was dirty and messy. I caught the bus to Providence and a taxi to my house. All was quiet, dark. I paid the driver and entered the house. I worried that I might startle Linda so I whispered her name from across the room. She stirred slightly.

"Linda." I put down my bag and sat on the edge of her side of the bed. I pushed her hair from her face, tucked it behind her ear. I always loved doing that. She never liked it.

"You're home," she said, her eyes still closed. She reached for my hand. "Are you tired?"

"Not so much. How is Will?"

"His fever actually broke, I think. I gave him some Tylenol anyway."

"Good. Should I look in on him?"

"No, let him sleep. You should come to bed."

"Actually, it's lunchtime for me. You go back to sleep. I'm going to make a sandwich."

"Okay."

"Linda," I said.

"Yes?"

"Nothing."

I sat at the table in the kitchen and waited for my tea water to boil. I was home. My family was asleep. My lover was three thousand miles away and I assumed she was sad. But I was at my house. I was sitting quietly in my kitchen while my children and my wife slept. And though I missed my lover, I was not sad. I was satisfied. I was different.

1979

The plane landed at LAX and we marched like doomed cattle to customs. We stopped at the restroom on the way and tried to get cleaned up. We did the best we could. Richard gave Tad one of his shirts and a pair of shorts. I put on a cleanish T-shirt and brushed off my jeans as best I could. I took off my boots and washed the soles in the sink.

"How do I look?" I asked.

"You look like a serial killer," Tad said.

"Great." I washed my hands and arms again, but I could not wash off the scratches and cuts.

Richard looked at the mirror. "I think this is about as good as it's going to get." He tightened his belt. "Probably best if we're not traveling together. What do you think?"

"Sounds right," I said. "Tad, go on out and get in line."

"We're going to be okay?" Richard said.

"I'm scared shitless. Here we are in our own fucking country and I'm scared to death."

"Nothing to be afraid of," Tad said.

"You can say that. You're white."

"Let's go," Richard said.

Tad walked on out.

"You first," I said.

Richard left the restroom and I remained. I looked at myself in the mirror. I couldn't believe what the man in there had done. My hands were shaking. I thought I saw my eye twitch. I was going to have to get myself under control before I walked up to that counter and handed over my passport. I took a few deep breaths, jumped up and down in front of my reflection. I tried to think of a tune to run through my head, something soothing, but all I could come up with was "My Favorite Things," but that turned from calm and simple to John Coltrane's frenetic, manic, and angry version. At first that agitated me, but I let it play freely in my head and suddenly I was breathing more evenly. If I couldn't appear clean, I could appear unruffled. An Indian or Pakistani man came into the restroom and gave me a long look before stepping quickly into a stall. I left to get in the queue.

Tad was well ahead of Richard in a folding line of passengers. I was at the very rear of another queue. Richard kept looking back at me and when he did I looked down or away, avoiding any eye contact that might have connected us or betrayed our connection. I didn't see Tad at the agent's window, but then I saw that he was on the far side waiting for Richard. They had passed through customs and I saw this as encouraging.

They had stepped down the hall before my turn with the agent to give us some separation. I pushed my passport forward.

"Mr. Pace," the heavyset man said. His cheeks were unusually rosy and with his pale skin and blue eyes he looked like an American flag.

I nodded.

"Only El Salvador?"

"That's correct."

"How long were you there?"

"Three nights."

"What was the purpose of your visit?" he asked.

I had of course been anticipating this question. "I'm a painter and I was down there looking around."

He looked at me. "Three days. Not a very long stay?"

"Four days, three nights," I said.

"A mess down there," he said.

"I didn't really know about all that stuff until I got there," I said. "Pretty stupid, I know."

He tapped on my passport with a finger and stared at me, at my face, my clothes. "Why don't you just wait right here for minute," he said. "Just a minute." He stepped out of his station and talked to another agent. They both looked at me.

My guy came back and picked up the phone. I couldn't hear what he was saying. He hung up. "Someone is going to come talk to you."

"Is there a problem?" I asked.

"You can talk to this gentleman." He pointed at the suited man who was approaching me.

The new man was short and I might have thought him well dressed had his suit fit better. He took my passport from the agent.

"Just back from El Salvador, Mr. Pace?"

"Yes."

"Would you come with me, please."

I walked with him. I glanced at Richard, but didn't catch his eyes.

"My name is Special Agent Douglas."

"Who do you work for?" I asked, feeling immediately sorry I had.

He ignored my question and opened a door, nodded for me to enter. It was a small, windowless room with a table and two chairs. It looked for the world like the interrogation rooms I'd seen in movies. "Have a seat, Mr. Pace."

"Is there something wrong?" I asked.

"Probably not. Should I think there's something wrong?"

"No." He reminded me of the unhelpful man in the American Embassy in San Salvador.

"Can you tell me why you were in El Salvador?"

"Like I told the agent out there, I'm a painter and was just looking around. I had some time and I thought a new place might help me work."

"So, you picked a place with a civil war?"

"I didn't know about that. I'm an artist and sometimes I just don't read the news."

"So what was it like down there?"

"Kind of scary right before we left," I said.

"We?"

"You know, the people on the plane."

"So, you were traveling alone."

"Yes."

He looked at my customs form. "Says here you live in Phila-delphia."

"That's correct."

"Yet you flew into Los Angeles."

"I was trying to get out of El Salvador. Like you said, there's a war going on down there."

"Did you meet anyone while you were in El Salvador?"

"What do you mean?"

"Did you make any new friends?" he asked.

"I met some people."

"Did you feel comfortable there?"

"Well, I don't speak Spanish, except for a few words."

"Yet, you got on just fine," he said.

"I'm glad to be home. Listen, am I in trouble?"

"Did you meet any Americans down there?"

"A couple, I guess."

"Any on the plane with you?"

"Yes, some reporter, but I don't know his name."

"I see."

"Can I go?"

"Someone waiting for you?"

I shook my head and relaxed into the seat.

"Did you see any violence?"

"No. Yes, sort of. I saw a tank."

"That must have been scary."

I nodded.

"Do you use drugs, Mr. Pace? The recreational kind."

"No. I do drink."

"Any plans to go back?"

"None."

"Would you like to go back?" He smiled at me, but I didn't know how to read him. "To El Salvador, I mean."

I laughed. "Not really."

"Why not?"

"Again, there's a civil war going on."

He laughed too. "What if you had a free trip?"

"Excuse me?"

"You say you were comfortable down there and you met some friends. I'm just wondering if you might want to visit again. If you had a ticket. Would it help your painting to go back?"

"I don't think so."

He pulled his upper lip tight across his teeth as if he was disappointed. He then reached into his jacket pocket and pulled out a photograph. He handed it to me. "Have you ever seen this man?"

It was the Bummer. He was younger, but I recognized him immediately. I looked at the picture for a few seconds. "He looks sort of familiar, but I don't think I know him. Who is he?"

"You didn't meet him down there?"

I shook my head. "Who is he?"

"His name is Bumgarner."

"Why would I have met him?"

"He's an American down there. You know how people run into each other. This guy, well, he's kind of a war criminal."

"I see. I didn't meet him. I don't remember seeing him."

"Where'd you go down there?" he asked. "You're an artist. You go to the museums? Were they open?"

"I don't much like museums. I just drove around the countryside. I liked the colors. Can I go now?"

"Yeah, you can go." He pushed his card toward me. There was only his name, Matt Douglas, and a number on it. No agency name. No address. "You call me if you decide you'd like to go back down there."

I picked up the card. "I'll do that. I can go?"

"You can go." He remained seated.

I stood and walked to the door.

"Think about it," he said without looking at me.

"You bet."

I walked out of the room and closed the door when I was on the other side. I was a wreck and I thought I understood the conversation I'd just had, but I couldn't believe it. I found my way out and found Tad and a near-crazed Richard waiting for me.

"Good god, what happened?" Richard asked.

"I don't know, but I think I just got recruited by the CIA."

"What the fuck?" Richard said. "Hey, why don't they want me?"

"I don't know, but I don't want to talk about it. I just want to go home."

House

The Avis car rental could have been in Cleveland or Boston, except the desk staff spoke perfect English. I collected my Nissan Sentra and drove into town. I found my hotel, the Hotel Villa Florencia Centro, a very nice place without a single rugged note. It was, as the name suggested, near the city center, though I didn't recognize the center at all. This was a place I had never been. For the life of me I could not recall the name of the hotel in which I had stayed in 1979, and neither could Richard, not that I wanted to be there. I needed to see, to feel only two places. I called Linda once I was in my room to let her know that I had arrived safely. We didn't say much. I walked around a bit, then returned to my room for a shower, a light room service dinner, and a decent night's sleep. I awoke early and studied my map. I had already marked the tiny speck that was Las Salinas. Finding my way this far had been easy enough, as the place of my bad dreams had turned into a popular equatorial paradise. Richard had had no desire to return and I did not blame him. Fact was, I wanted to be alone in El Salvador, for whatever reason I wanted to be there.

The remarkable thing about where I was now driving was that it was not remarkable in any way. Strip malls, functional glass and steel office buildings, fast food restaurants, many of the brands I knew. I drove out of the city just the way I imagined I had driven so many years ago, into the same mountains that I had no reason and certainly not the power to recognize. Through the city and into the country and into the mountains I never felt unsafe. Even when I was lost I never felt lost. There had been a recent fire in the mountains and though I could not have claimed that it altered anything that I might have found familiar, the charred ground and blackened trees reminded me that landscapes are ever changing.

The fire had changed that mountain and my time in that country had forever changed me.

What I thought might have been the cantina in which we had spent a night, in which I had met the awful Carlos, was now a burned-out cinder-block shell. However, some miles beyond it, on a now-developed road that I didn't believe had been there before, was a nice resort with nicely parallel-parked rental cars and nicely dressed white Americans and Europeans. I stopped there for a rest and a bite and to orient myself. I talked to a tall man just a little older than me who was watering the hanging plants on the terrace where I sat.

"It's beautiful here," I said.

He looked at me, the yellow watering can hanging from his big hand. He didn't speak English.

"*Hermoso*," I said.

"*Sí.*"

I pointed west. "*Las Salinas, ya está.*"

He shook his head and pointed slightly more north.

That surprised me, but I believed him. There was no reason not to.

"*Por qué quieres ir allí?*"

I didn't understand him, but I heard the word *why*.

"I just want to see it," I said, stupidly, knowing that he had no English. So I shrugged.

That seemed to satisfy him. "*Vaya con dios*," he said.

"*Gracias.*"

I sat at the table for a while longer, watched the tourists from many places sip their drinks and eat their authentic dishes. I finished my American hamburger, paid my tab, and got back into my car.

I followed my map and the twisting road, remembering that I had come to this village thirty years earlier on what was barely a wagon trail. This way in, whatever way it was, was well worked and unmaintained asphalt. I came to a collection of simple houses. Satellite dishes sat on top of a couple of them. There was a tiny convenience store with an old-fashioned soda pop cooler wedged between a house and what I took to be a public building. There were no signs.

I parked and walked into the public building. It smelled like a bathroom and looked a little like one with its institutional green walls. There was a waist-high counter but there was no one behind it. Instead, a young woman sat in the only chair in what might have been a waiting area.

"*Hola,*" she said.

"*Hola.* Is this Las Salinas?"

She nodded. "You are looking for Las Salinas?"

"Yes. *Sí.*"

"We can speak English," she said.

"Thank you." I looked around. "What is this building?"

"We don't know yet," she said. "The government built it for us, but we don't know what to do with it."

"Looks like a police station," I said.

"If we only had a policeman."

I smiled. "You don't want one of those."

"Why do you come to Las Salinas?" she asked.

"I'm just a tourist."

"Tourists don't come to Las Salinas. Tourists go to Lake Coatepeque. Tourists go to the Basílica Nuestra Señora de Guadalupe. You might even go to the Ruta de las Flores. Tourists don't come to Las Salinas."

"So, who comes to Las Salinas?" I asked.

"People who live in Las Salinas."

"Well, I was here many years ago and I just wanted to see it again."

"See what? When were you here?"

"Before you were born."

"I am not so young," she said.

"Why are you sitting in here?" I asked.

"No reason. There's a chair in here. Trying to figure out what this place is supposed to be. Maybe I want to be a policeman."

I nodded, looked around, at the windows in the front, at the empty shelves behind the counter. "I was here in 1979," I told her and watched her expression change. She didn't become cool or hard, but confused, I think. "I'm not completely sure this is where I was. I was told it was Las Salinas."

"That was when the war started," she said. "Are you a soldier?"

"Look at me. I'm an old man."

"Not so old. But there are old soldiers. Were you a soldier then? You were not old back then."

"I'm a painter."

"You're an American." She didn't like that fact, I could tell. "Were you a soldier?"

"I was a painter then too."

"There is nothing here," she said. "There has never been anything here."

"You're here," I said.

"True."

"My name is Kevin."

"Betty."

"How is it that you speak English?"

"School. I went to school in San Salvador. I came back because my grandmother is dying."

"I'm sorry." I leaned against the wall. My legs felt suddenly tired.

"That's why I came back. What about you? Why have you come back?" She was suspicious, but she didn't know why she was.

"I don't really know why I'm here. I don't even know if I'm in the right place." I studied her young, high-cheekboned but wise face and decided to simply tell her. "Thirty years ago I was here or someplace just like here and I saw a terrible thing. I didn't actually see it happen, but I saw a little girl. She had been murdered. I had never seen a dead person, certainly not a dead child. Her father was there. She had a little brother."

"You saw this girl killed?"

I shook my head. "Like I said, I didn't see it happen. I saw her after. I saw her father. I will never forget it."

She stood and looked out the window. "Would you come with me?"

"Pardon?"

"Come with me," she repeated.

"Where are we going?"

"Just come with me."

I followed her and we walked past the grouping of houses, around a bend, the road turning from asphalt to gravel, to another huddle of small houses. These houses on the deteriorating road were incongruously nicer or at least better kept than the other houses on the better road. The sky was starting to cloud over.

"Wait here," she said. She stepped onto the porch of a yellow house, then turned back to me. "You wait?"

I nodded.

She went inside. I kicked at a couple of light-colored stones appearing to float over the darker gravel. A light rain began to fall, but I remained outside the house, in the middle of the road. I blurred my vision and stared at the rocks on the road and found it looked like a Pollock. I heard the door open.

I turned to see the young woman step out with a man my age or slightly older behind her. He was wearing new jeans, stiff and rolled above his sneakers, and a plaid flannel shirt. I stared at the man's face and he stared at mine. He walked to me, put his arms around me, and cried. I cried, also.

1979

There is a cruelty in abstraction. It cuts into flesh. It relies on our fear of mortality for its meaning. The way it disturbs, distresses is meant to undermine some illusion of duration, of time controlled, even simply perceived. My paintings were abstract and splashed with guilt as much as paint, scratched with shame as much as with the knife or spatula. Back in Philadelphia I discovered bad dreams and fitful sleep. I locked myself away to explore those abstractions. My isolation wore well as I was an artist and artists were supposed to be moody and at least occasionally reclusive. The paintings I made I could just barely look at. I drank. When I emerged from my bed, so to speak, and went to my studio and revealed my paintings at my review, no one said a word. My professors, one after another, quietly, privately gave me nods of approval, then backed away as if something was wrong with me. They had no idea.

Linda, during my down time, called several times a week. It was clear that I was hurting her, but I couldn't bring myself to be near her, anyone. I lived with Richard and he knew what had happened and I barely saw him once every couple of days. He and Linda bonded over concern for me, though he never told her what happened in San Salvador. He told her about nearly everything, but not about the dead child or about the little man I had killed. Excuse me, murdered. I drank.

I wanted to be with her but I felt trapped inside myself. When she reached for me, I didn't know how to reach back. But she persisted. She came to my review, joined me near the end of the show in front of the largest canvas.

"It's amazing," she said.

"I'm sorry I've been so, so—"

"It's okay. You've been working. It's good."

"They're shit," I said. "I've been offered a show. They're shit and I've been offered a show."

"I've missed you."

"I've missed you, too. Want to grab a bite?"

"Please."

We sat in a Japanese restaurant and ate sushi. I drank hot sake. She told me what she liked about the paintings. I cannot say that she was right or wrong or even whether what she was saying made sense, but it soothed me. She told me she didn't like one of the canvases and I asked why.

"It's a good thing that I don't like it," she said. "If it wasn't working against something, some likeness or idea, I wouldn't be able to find it difficult."

"You know what I think?" I asked.

"What?"

"I think you're a lot smarter than I am."

"I don't know about that."

"I'm just a dumb painter. I put color on canvas."

We sat and ate some more.

"Are you feeling better?" she asked. "I was worried about you."

"I'm better now. I'm glad we found Richard's brother, but I didn't want to see a war. Or an almost war."

"You're home now."

Linda made me feel safe, normal. I wanted my life to be safe, normal. We ate together that night and every night for several months. We became a habit. Safe and normal. And I drank.

House

His name was Emberto Rodriguez. I had not had children that day in 1979 and so could not fully understand the depth of his grief. But now I did. We spoke only of the weather, of the rain that fell every day, of the changes in their country, about the mysterious public building. Betty translated.

A young man in his thirties came into the house with a woman, his wife. He was confused to find an American in his father's home. I shook his hand and imagined I saw in him the four-year-old Luis. His name was Arturo. His wife's name was Elsa and she seemed more distrustful than any of them.

Arturo was very quiet. He listened but did not join in the small talk. I kept looking at his eyes, wondering if he might remember the moment we shared, the hand, but I never had the sense that he did. I recalled how my children remembered so little from before the age of six. It could have been argued that what they did remember was there only because of familial repetition.

"Things are much better since the war," Betty translated Emberto.

"I can see that," I said. "Sadly, my country remains exactly the same."

Betty translated and they all laughed, perhaps nervously, perhaps with no understanding of my joke.

"Betty tells me you're trying to figure out how to use your new building," I said.

Emberto shook his head. "The money they spend does not make sense."

I nodded. "A doctor could use it as a clinic," I said.

"That would be good," Emberto said through Betty, it being clear that it was her answer also.

The sound of a sudden downpour quieted us for a moment. I

looked out at the rain and remembered that day. I think Emberto did as well. If Arturo didn't recall it, I believed he felt it.

I was invited to stay for dinner.

"No, I have to go," I told them. I stood and shook Emberto's hand. We shared a look, but didn't hug again.

I nodded good-bye to Arturo and his wife.

"I will walk you back to your car," Betty said.

Arturo followed us out. He stopped me with a hand on my shoulder. I turned and reached out to shake. He said nothing, in Spanish or English.

Betty and I walked back along the wet gravel. Some yards away I looked to see that Arturo was still watching.

"Thank you for taking me there," I said to Betty.

"The story of Emberto's daughter is a terrible one. The village will always remember it."

"What was her name?" I asked.

"Her name was Lavada."

"That's a beautiful name. I should have asked that thirty years ago. I should have asked it back at the house."

"No, you did fine."

I looked at Betty, but she was not looking at me. "Thank you," I said.

Betty stopped walking. "Would you like to visit Lavada's grave?"

This took me by surprise and it occurred to me that this was probably why I had come. "Yes, I would."

"So, why were you here back then?" Betty asked. She led me left through the broken rails of a wooden fence and onto a dirt path.

"Stupid stuff," I said. "My friend's brother got into trouble and we came to find him."

"You are a good friend," she said.

"I don't know about that. Who knows why I really came. I came to this country like it didn't matter. I had no idea what was going on here and I didn't care once I was here. It was a bad time. We just happened onto Emberto after, after—"

"Emberto is a good man. Arturo hardly ever speaks."

"He was pretty young to see what he saw," I said. "I have children. I can't imagine if they had to see that sort of violence."

"You're right. It was a bad time."

"What about Arturo's mother?"

"She died before Lavada was killed. She was sick. That's the story I heard." She stopped us at a lone grave. There was a wrought iron fence around it. There was a nice headstone. The grave was between an old storage shed recently painted red and a new barn that was unpainted. I didn't recognize the place at all.

"I helped dig this grave," I said, more to myself than to Betty. I turned and tried to imagine the path in which I had found Lavada's body but everything seemed turned around.

Betty said nothing.

I looked around one more time. "Well, thank you," I said.

"Do you want to say a prayer?" she asked.

"No, thank you."

"You don't believe in God?" she asked.

"No," I said. "I don't mind if you do, but I don't."

"Neither do I," she said.

This surprised me. "Why did you ask me if I wanted to pray?"

"Usually people who do things like this are believers. You came all this way like you need to repent."

"I guess that's right," I said. "It must seem odd."

"A little. That's not a bad thing."

"Thanks for saying that," I said.

Betty led me back to my Nissan Sentra.

House

I married Linda. She was happy. I was content. We set about life.
Years passed and my arrested development stalled our having children. But all of us finally develop and I did too and so we did have
children. I loved both my daughter and my son. I felt normal. I felt
safe. But the dreams persisted. I drank too much on occasion but
was always excused, disappeared on occasion but was forgiven.

House

The drive back to San Salvador was clearer, but it felt longer. I didn't know what I had achieved by my visit, though for some reason I felt better. I arrived at my hotel at two in the morning. I was starving, but there was nothing to be done about that. I did not go up to my room, but sat in the deserted lobby. The night clerk asked me several times if I needed anything and then finally left me alone. At four, before any sign of morning showed, I left the hotel and walked the wet streets. I followed the Calle Poniente east until I came to the Catedral Metropolitana and remembered that I had been east and south of there. Everything continued to look completely different from what I thought I remembered. But as testimony to the unreliability of memory, I smelled a brewery and realized the breeze was coming from the north. In my mind I realized I was walking with Linda. I could hear her voice telling me that I was a good man. She did actually say that to me on occasion, out of the blue, at times when I was revisiting the event that made me question my goodness. She didn't know, but she knew and I had always taken her for granted. I was broken and felt unworthy of love, oddly not of being loved, but of loving. To love seemed so special and how could I achieve that? I walked north, but found no brewery and then the odor was gone, just like that, as if it had never been in the air. I was standing in front of a Mister Donut shop when I looked up the street and saw the defunct tanks of a brewery. I remembered the tanks. I did not remember the street. The Mister Donut had just opened and its bright lights spilled out into the still nearly dark street. As if in concert, the sun came out and made everything daytime. As everything became daytime, my desire to find the spot of my crime evaporated. My Linda said to me that I was a good and decent man and I believed her. I did not need to relive that death. Fact was, I did not need to relive anything.

House

Linda was cleaning the kitchen when I walked into the house through the back door. It was late afternoon but still bright out.

"I'll take care of that," I said.

"You scared me," she said, resting a hand on the sink.

"I'm sorry."

"When did you land?"

"Just a few hours ago. Where are the guys?" I put my bag down, stepped closer to hug her.

"Both of them have sleepovers. How about that?"

"How are you?"

"I'm okay. I've just made tea."

"That sounds perfect."

We sat at the table and stared at the pot while the tea steeped. "So, did you find what you were looking for?

"I don't know. I didn't know what I was looking for." Sitting there with her right then I realized that telling her the secret I should have told her so long ago was not going to bring us any closer and probably wouldn't make sense anyway. All of that was in another world and another life. There were all sorts of things I could tell her, confess to, but why?

"I was so angry with you," she said.

"I know." I was pleased she had used the past tense. "I screwed up."

"Not just about April," she said. "I've been angry for years. You've just never been here."

I listened. Before I might have become defensive, perhaps even hurt, but not now. She poured the tea. She was thirty years older than she was when we first met. She was slightly heavier. Her face was interestingly lined. Her hair was mostly gray. She had never been more beautiful than she was as she poured that tea. And I

loved her. I understood that I had always loved her and I was so sad
that I had never allowed her to feel that love.

I was about to say I was sorry, but I was done with apologies,
pointless apologies, empty words. Instead I said, "I want you to see
something."

"Okay."

"Come with me."

"Where are we going?"

I took Linda's hand and walked her out the back door toward
the shed. I could feel the muscles in her hand tense. I said nothing. I
unlocked the door. "I should have let you in here a long time ago."
I opened the studio. I let her walk in in front of me and I switched
on the lights. It was another world, the lights flooding everything
inside, the covered windows keeping out everything else. Linda
stood in front of the painting, moved slowly to the middle of it. I
stood behind her.

"So much blue," she said. "So much blue."

"Now you know everything."

"So much blue."

PERCIVAL EVERETT is Distinguished Professor of English at the University of Southern California. His most recent books include *James*, *Dr. No* (finalist for the NBCC Award for Fiction and winner of the PEN/Jean Stein Book Award), *The Trees* (finalist for the Booker Prize and the PEN/Faulkner Award for Fiction), *Telephone* (finalist for the Pulitzer Prize), *So Much Blue*, *Erasure*, and *I Am Not Sidney Poitier*. He has received the NBCC Ivan Sandrof Life Achievement Award and the Windham Campbell Prize from Yale University. *American Fiction*, the feature film based on his novel *Erasure*, was released in 2023. He lives in Los Angeles with his wife, the writer Danzy Senna, and their children.

The text of *So Much Blue* is set in Dante MT Pro. Design and composition by Bookmobile Design & Digital Publisher Services, Minneapolis, Minnesota. Manufactured by Versa Press on acid-free, 30 percent postconsumer wastepaper.